KILLINOIS!

FRANK YOUNG

ISBN-10: 147769661X
EAN-13: 9781477696613
Library of Congress Control Number: 2012911223
CreateSpace, North Charleston, SC

To Justine,
my goddess of virtue

1

Morning sunlight glittered off the surface of the water. Sandstone cliffs rose high over the river. Birds called out from the scrub oaks and pines along the banks. Far in the distance, a barge drifted along with the slow current. The sky was blue, without a cloud, and the sun blazed into the heavy Midwest summer air. An engine whined downriver. The engine grew louder, and a watercraft appeared on the horizon. The river surface was smooth. Tiny insects danced on the water. A girl in a red life vest was riding a Jet Ski, her long black hair whipping behind her. She was going high speed in a straight line, smiling with her lips closed, sitting up straight. She was young and tan, alone with the sun and the water and her machine.

A rustling in the bushes on the far side of the river, and a nearly invisible line rose up several feet out of the water. Droplets shimmered across the clear line as it straightened out from one bank across to an island mid-river. The girl maintained her speed, lifting her head up to fully catch the sun's rays on her round cheeks. Ahead, the line grew taut, and water droplets burst into the air. The machine rocketed toward the line. The engine sang, and the girl beamed. She barreled ahead. The line tore through her neck.

The girl's head flew off. Blood showered out as it spun in the sky, fanning an arc of red mist in all directions. The watercraft kept racing, a headless teenager gripping the throttle. Her head landed in the river twenty feet away with a deep plop, sunk below, and then popped back up and gently floated down with the current. The line slackened back into the water. The engine died as the body dropped backward, pulling the machine's emergency switch by the lanyard attached to the girl's life vest. Deep red blood poured out of the black gaping hole above her shoulders as the Jet Ski drifted sideways with the current. The body and craft slowly followed the head down the river, and birds resumed singing in the trees along the shore.

2

The black Jeep Wrangler blasted south down Highway 39. The soft top was down, the doors were stuffed in the back, and three boys yelled over the howling wind and the Rolling Stones.

"We still need ice," shouted Scott Hey, the driver. He was muscular, with a thick neck and a buzz cut. One of his eyelids drooped lower than the other. He glanced in the rearview mirror for cops and then jerked up to ninety.

"Fuck ice," said Jerrod from the back seat, "we need more beer."

"What?" shouted Scott.

"We need more fucking beer, man!" Jerrod yelled again, leaning in between his two best friends. Peter Rockwood rode shotgun, bouncing his head to "Gimme Shelter" and watching the tall rows of corn fly by. Peter had dark brown eyes, brownish black hair, and a slight overbite. Scott elbowed Jerrod in the chest, knocking him back.

"We've got three cases of Coors Light," Scott said. "Plus the girls are bringing some. How much do you fucking need?"

"More!" Jerrod yelled back. Jerrod's long legs barely fit in the cramped back seat. His eyes were set far apart behind long reddish bangs, currently whipping in the wind.

"Plus we've got two bottles of So-Co and the Jack Daniels," Peter said.

"We'll only have two cases by the time we get to the marina," Jerrod shouted from the back, and then tossed an empty beer can out the side of the Jeep. "Pete, would you be so kind as to beer me, you fucking fag?"

"Here you go, shitbird," Peter said as he handed him a semicold one out of the cooler under his seat. "I think I'm about ready myself." He opened another and took a deep drink. "What is it about noon-beers on a Thursday that tastes so fucking good?"

"The alcohol, you fucking lush!" Jerrod yelled.

The song faded away, and Scott turned off the radio. "So here we are, my friends—about a half hour away from one big-ass houseboat with our name on it."

"Motherfuckin' houseboat!" Jerrod yelled.

"We've got more booze than we know what to do with. We've got mister Johnny college sitting over here drinking noon-beers," Scott yelled. Peter gave him the finger. "We don't have to go back to our no good fucking jobs until Monday."

"Fuckin' A!" Jerrod said.

"And I think I am ready for my next beer," Scott concluded. He tossed his empty out the driver's side, and Peter handed him a new one.

"Don't forget about the fucking talent," Jerrod yelled. "Hot-ass bitches on a motherfucking houseboat!"

"Watch that 'bitches' shit," Peter shot back. "One of those bitches is mine remember."

"Oh yeah, how could I forget," Jerrod said. "Oh Petey, I'll wait for you while you're away at college. Petey, don't worry about me, I'm all alone back in Dixon, and I've got nothing to do tonight but swim around naked in my parent's pool."

"Yo, shut the fuck up, bitch!" Peter yelled. "I swear to God, seriously. Shut the fuck up about the pool, all right!"

"Easy!" Scott said, turning the radio back up. "Dude, you should have been there. Seriously, that party was insane. Naked chicks everywhere. I think there were like thirty chicks naked in that pool."

"Fuck that was great," Jerrod said.

"Fuck you both. Fuck you both up your stupid asses," Peter said, and then tossed his empty beer can back at Jerrod. "Which one of you pussies is ready for round three?"

3

Maggie Dymerski shifted her red Pontiac Sunbird into park and killed the ignition. "Pure Morning" from Placebo shut off with the engine. She took the final drag from her cigarette and then flicked the butt out the window. Tapping her fingertips on the top of her steering wheel, she peered across the parking lot of the small town grocery store.

"Is this the right store?" Beth Miller asked, sitting across from her. Beth was tall and slender, with platinum blond hair and light blond eyebrows. She had on cutoff jean shorts and a black bikini top.

"Yeah, Jack's Grocery—that's what he said," Maggie answered. "Come on. Let's go in you skanks." Maggie and Beth stepped out of the car at the same time, and Beth's younger sister Jen climbed out of the backseat. Jen was shorter than Beth, and her dirty blond dreadlocks were in sharp contrast to her sister's shoulder-length hair. She wore a light yellow summer dress. All three were well tanned from sunbathing at Maggie's pool. Maggie's eyes darted across the front of the store, looking for a VW microbus. Black D&G sunglasses covered her round freckled face. Her brunet hair was back in a ponytail, and she wore a low-cut, red tank top with soccer shorts. A few old people shuffled out of the store carrying loads of food in brown paper bags. As they passed by, an old woman walked out of the store with a bag slightly overflowing with packaged meat.

"There you go Jen," Beth said. "You joining them for the barbecue?"

"Ha ha, so funny," Jen replied. "Are you joining them to go suck some donkey dick?"

Beth stuck out her long tongue at her sister as they walked through the entrance. Maggie suddenly stopped. Jen walked into Beth. All three froze. Standing in front of them was a group of men, huddled around the cash register. The men looked like old farmers, or fishermen, in overalls and dark blue worker shirts and baseball hats. Their skin was weather-worn and smudged with grease or dirt. All of them turned silent as soon as the girls took a few steps in. The men stared.

"Okay," Maggie said, taking one step forward. The locals continued to gawk. "We are going to buy some groceries now." She paused, waiting for a reaction. She took another step, and their eyes followed her. She stepped backward.

"Whatever," Beth said. "Weirdos." The three walked briskly toward the nearest aisle, and the men watched them walk away.

"Oh shit," Maggie said, "we need a basket."

"You go get it," Beth said.

"No, you go get it," she whispered. Some of the men were leaning into the aisle to observe.

"You chicken shits," Jen said. "I'll get the basket." She walked back up the aisle and scanned the front. "Of course," she said. The baskets were stacked next to the window where the old men were standing. She marched up until she was standing face to face with one of them. She forced a smile.

"Pardon me sir," she said in her best phony Southern accent. "Could you be a dear and hand me one of them little old baskets?"

None of the group said a word. They stared open-mouthed at Jen. One of the men nearest the stack reached behind him, without taking his eyes off her, grasped the plastic handle, lifted a basket out, and handed it to her. Jen dropped the smile.

"What's wrong?" she asked. "Why are you all staring at me?"

"Young lady," one with no teeth finally spoke, "we've been meeting here a long, long time. This is what you call the good old boys club, I guess." He grinned, and the rest of the group seemed to relax. "Watching you walk into our little store here is like, well, it's like heaven for me and the cousins." They all nodded in agreement. Jen grinned nervously.

"Okay, then…thanks." She held up the basket, turned on her heels, and walked away. She felt their eyes on her body until she rounded the corner.

"What the hell was that all about?" Maggie asked.

"Oh, my God!" Jen said. "Fucking freaks."

Beth and Maggie dumped some Gatorade and string cheese in the basket. The three walked together through the aisles, picking up their supplies. When they rounded the end of the snack aisle, a short store employee almost ran into them with his cart. His face was covered with acne. He looked directly at Maggie's breasts and then turned to stare at Beth's bikini top.

"Hey," Maggie said, "up here, fresh." He jerked his head up and looked at her through thick glasses.

"Doesn't anyone in this town know it's not polite to stare?"

The clerk blushed red, grunted, and scurried past them, spilling some bags of cookies as he escaped.

"Now we really need to get the fuck out of here," Beth said.

"We still have to pay."

"Fuck. Can't we just run out? They couldn't catch us."

"Don't worry, bitches," Maggie sighed. "We've got plastic, and we've got tits. We are unstoppable." She marched toward the front, and the sisters followed behind. Beth glanced back to catch the young clerk peering at them from behind the opposite end of the aisle. She put one finger up to her lips and smiled. His eyes widened. She lifted her hip slightly and spanked herself. His jaw dropped. She blew him a kiss, and then his head disappeared around the corner. She hurried to catch up with her friends.

An overweight woman checked them out at the front. She took her time ringing up each item, looking at the product and looking at the girls. Her arm fat jiggled each time she reached for something new. Behind her, the men mumbled to themselves and periodically shot glances. The woman had wrinkled lips and a faint mustache.

"Pack of Marlboro Lights too, please," Maggie said.

"We don't sell cigarettes here—have to buy them at customer service," the woman said, breathing heavily.

"Where's customer service?"

"Customer service's closed."

"If it's closed, then I can't buy cigarettes."

"Guess not."

"And you can't help me out?"

"Nope."

"Thanks so much."

The woman held up a bag of chips and looked into Maggie's eyes. She glared. Then she put the chips in a grocery bag and smiled.

"You're welcome. Thanks for shopping at Jack's. Have a nice day."

4

"Ugh!" Maggie slammed the trunk of her car down. "What a bitch!"

"This whole place gives me the creeps," Beth said. "Is that like a bad sign or something?"

"Well, luckily we aren't staying here, we will be out on the river," Jen said.

"Yeah," Beth said. "Duh. You don't think those freaks in there have boats?"

"Duh yourself, bitch. You scared?"

"I think that's Jacob," Maggie said, pointing at a rusty white VW microbus pulling into the parking lot. She waved, and the driver waved back.

"So does Peter know about him yet?" Beth said.

"No, why?" Maggie said.

"Just wondering," Beth smirked.

Jacob rolled up next to the girls and rolled down the window. The engine screeched as he parked. Maggie ran up to greet him as he got out. He was several years older than her, tall and thin, with black hair pulled back into a ponytail. His cheeks had several days' worth of stubble, and he sported a pointed goatee on his chin. He wore a faded purple tie-dyed t-shirt, dark green shorts, and was barefoot.

"Maggs, good to see you, girl," Jacob said. Maggie gave him a warm embrace and pecked him on the cheek. She held his hand and walked him back over to the sisters.

"Beth, Jen, you remember Jacob, right?"

"Hey," Beth said coolly.

"'Sup," Jen said.

"Nice dreads," Jacob said. Maggie frowned.

"Thanks. Nice bus," Jen said.

"So cool of you to come down this weekend," Jacob said. "I can't believe you all actually rented a houseboat, you're going to have the best trip ever."

"Only weekend we could get," Maggie said. "All the other dates were booked. We're lucky to get one, actually."

"Yeah, they do pretty good business renting those things, for sure."

"How can you stand living here?" Beth asked.

"What do you mean?"

"It was like…every one of the people inside that grocery store was staring at us the entire time."

Jacob paused, looking up in the air. Then his eyes met Beth's. "Oh, don't let the locals spook you," he said. "I bet they were staring. You're probably the prettiest things they've seen in years."

"So Jacob," Maggie said, and swung his arm by the hand, "before we get out on the water, you think you can hook a sister up?"

Jacob smirked. "Right down to business, huh? Yeah, I got what you want. You want to give it a try first?"

Maggie looked at her friends and then back at Jacob. "We've got a little time before our friends get in. Yeah, sounds like fun."

"Bertha has room for one more," Jacob said, patting the side of his bus. "The other two will have to follow behind until we get there."

"Get where?" Jen asked.

"Um, down by the river, before the bridge there are a few picnic tables. Usually it's pretty quiet down there."

Maggie tossed her keys to Beth, smiled at Jacob, and climbed in through the open driver's side door of the microbus. Jacob watched as she crawled like a cat across the cracked leather seat. She bounced into the passenger side and then beckoned Jacob by curling her finger. Jacob smiled at the sisters and then pulled himself into the bus and shut the door.

"Don't lose us," Beth said. "I've never driven in Utica before."

"No worries," Jacob said. "You can't get lost. Trust me." He turned on the engine, sending a high-pitched whine back through the parking lot.

"Should we ditch them?" he asked Maggie.

"No, of course not." Maggie slapped his arm. "They have the money."

"Just kidding, girl." He pressed the power button on the Audiovox tape deck that was mounted on top of the dashboard. Maggie pulled up one foot on her seat and looked out the window at her friends as they drove forward. Drums and guitar rang through the speakers.

"Coming around, coming around, coming around," multiple voices chanted to the music. She watched Jacob sing along under his breath.

"What are we listening to—Phish?"

"No," he said. "Dead, man."

"It all sounds the same to me."

"This was one of the best concerts ever. Winterland 1977. The girls were wild back then."

"Like you were there?" Maggie asked, suddenly losing interest as she looked behind her. The back of the bus was taken up completely by a bed. A pile of mismatched blankets partially covered the bare mattress. Brown and orange plaid curtains shaded the windows.

Jacob glanced behind him and then looked back toward the road. "Too bad you are out on the river this weekend instead of with me, we could put that to good use."

"Whatever," Maggie laughed. "My boyfriend wouldn't like that too much."

"That didn't seem to stop you at Matt's party."

"Totally different. You caught me at a moment of weakness," Maggie said. She watched the old houses on her side of the street turn to storefronts as they drove through the downtown. A few tourists were peering into a gift store window. An old man with a mutt sat on a bench. He wore a windbreaker pulled up over his head. He made eye contact with her as they drove by. She turned away.

"And that's why you can't stop thinking about me, right?"

"Or, that you have the best weed in the state."

"So you're using me."

"You love it."

"You're right," he said. "Use me and abuse me." The downtown was behind them after only a few blocks. As they approached the bridge over the river, Jacob turned off to the right. Beth and Jen followed close behind. They took a wide loop down around to the frontage road.

"It was really sweet of you to help us put together this weekend. We all needed to get away from Dixon so bad. My mom is driving me fucking nuts."

"My pleasure," Jacob said. "You will love it out on the water. Smoke a little grass, drink a little booze, listen to some tunage. Maybe that friend of yours Beth will even lose her big V."

"Yeah right," Maggie said. "Beth's no virgin. She was the biggest slut in our class."

"Oh. Jen then?"

"Why?" Maggie said, leaning away from him.

Jacob furrowed his brow. "Didn't you tell me one of your friends back there was still a virgin?"

"I don't recall. You wouldn't have heard that from me."

"You guys were teasing her at that house party. Something about daddy's girl or promise rings?"

"I guess I don't remember," Maggie said. "If I told you at the party, I probably said a lot of things."

"So is she?"

"Jen is still a virgin, yes. Don't say anything. What do you care?"

"Just wondering," he said, holding the steering wheel with both hands. The wheel was almost horizontal like a spinning plate balanced on a pole. "They are Irish twins, right?"

"Yes." Maggie crossed her arms and looked back out the window.

"Don't you think it's funny how they are so close in age, same parents, same upbringing. One of them turns out to be a slut, and the other keeps her virginity all through high school? Siblings are interesting."

"Don't call my friend a slut. Can we change the subject please?"

"Sorry, that's what you called her." He waited for a response. "What am I talking about? I ramble on sometimes. Who cares, right?"

"You seem overly interested in my friends," Maggie said. "And you've got this hottie riding with you right here."

"Yes, indeed I do." He pulled the van up to a grove of pine trees in a small gravel lot. He shut of the engine, turned off the Dead, and squeezed Maggie's thigh. "You're the one with the boyfriend, remember," he said. "I'm here for you, whenever you need me, and whatever you need me for, and I don't care about your friends." He leaned in for a kiss, but Maggie popped open the door latch and spilled out into the warm morning air.

"Don't we have to meet the idiots soon?" Beth asked, sitting behind the wheel of Maggie's car.

"The marina is on the other side of the bridge," Jacob answered. "No hurries, man." He tiptoed barefoot across the gravel and leaned up against Jen's side of the car. "You gals like to party?"

"Hell yeah," Jen said. The two exited the Sunbird and followed Jacob to the picnic table by the water.

Maggie stood back a moment with her arms folded. She didn't know what exactly, but she had that feeling—that feeling like when she was at school and knew she had forgotten something but couldn't remember what. She looked behind her and then up above at the highway. No one around, and no one could see them from the road. She watched Jacob joking with Jen, and she became momentarily embarrassed, realizing she was a little jealous. The feeling quickly faded.

"Jacob, don't even think about lighting up that joint without me," she said. She walked over and wedged herself between him and her friends. Jen and Beth both scooted over a few inches. Jacob leaned in and hugged her. She smiled at Jen, took the joint Jacob was offering her, and lit it with her Zippo.

The four took turns passing the weed. They watched the brown water, wide and shallow, lapping against the mud banks. White herons stood far out in the middle of the river. Great cumulus clouds soared high above the river. The pine needles smelled like camp to Maggie. She felt a warm pressure in her eyes. She laughed.

"What's so funny?" Beth asked.

"Thinking of something. Nothing," she said. "Something…nothing." They all laughed.

"So are you joining us this weekend?" Jen asked, looking at Jacob.

"I wish," Jacob said, "but I am needed elsewhere unfortunately." He gazed out at the river, lifting his hairy chin. "You see, sweetheart, every year, on this weekend, my friends all get together, and we throw the biggest party around. Think Woodstock meets Lollapalooza."

"So why aren't we going to that?" Jen asked Maggie.

"Yeah," Maggie said. "Aren't we invited?"

Jacob stood up and took a few steps toward the riverbank. "Private party, I'm afraid. I think you would have a great time, but these friends are pretty exclusive."

"So where is it?" Maggie said.

"Can't say."

"When is it?" Beth said.

"Starts tonight. Goes for three days."

"What's so great about it?" Jen said.

"Everything," Jacob said. "Drugs. Music. Art. The people. It's one great big family, all living at the same time, you know."

"We want to go!" Beth said. "Who doesn't want to see three hot teenage—legal, I might add—bombshells at their party? It's not really a party without us."

"Look, I'm sorry I brought it up, all right? No party—forget I said it. Besides, you've got a houseboat. Wouldn't you lose the deposit or something?"

"Mom's credit card number and a fake ID," Maggie said.

"Well still, you're going to have way more fun on the river. You're not all really into the hippie scene anyway, right?"

"True."

"You've got a big bag a weed for your weekend," Jacob said.

"Also true."

"You brought some high school studs along to drool all over you the whole time, right?"

"Hey, Peter's in college," Maggie said.

"Well there you go. Ivy League boys smoke up more than anyone. So that's why," he paused, "I won't be joining you this weekend. I've got plans. But maybe I'll sneak out if I can, swim up in the dead of night, sneak up onto your boat"—he jabbed a finger under Maggie's arm—"and get ya!"

"Ahh!" Maggie jumped. "None of that, none of that. You call my cell if you are coming out. We've got enough local freaks to be worried about. Anyone sneaks up on the boat—they are going to get fucked up."

"Cell phone isn't going to work out on the water," Jacob said.

"What?" Beth asked. "What carrier?"

"Doesn't matter. ET not gonna phone home out there."

"Well, smoke signal or something. It's too bad you aren't taking us to that party."

"Oh Jesus, man, the party, the party. Just relax, ladies, don't worry about it. No hurries. No worries."

"So what's the party for?" Jen asked, fiddling with one of her dreads.

"To party."

"Yeah, loser, but why? You say every year this weekend—what's the occasion?"

Jacob sat back down and lit a second joint. He took a long drag, held it in, and then exhaled. The smoke billowed out from his lips.

"Summer solstice," he finally said, coughing. He offered the joint to Jen, who took it and took a drag.

"Is that like the astrological thing, or like some pagan thing?" Maggie asked.

"Yes, both actually," Jacob smiled. "Tomorrow is the longest day of the year for this part of the world. People throughout history have celebrated the equinox and the solstice. The days coincide with harvests and planting and life and death and rebirth."

"That's some heavy shit," Jen said.

"Yeah, pretty fucking sweet," Jacob said. "Before the Christian holidays, the ancient tribes would worship the things that were real to them in their lives. Things like the moon and the sun and stars and water."

"So is that what you are all going to do—worship the river?"

"No, not really. Just celebrating nature in general. Knowing that thousands of years ago, people were dancing around naked, making sacrifices, blessing their food supply, cursing their enemies—all around this same day. It's like a ritual. Back in the day, all the village women thought summer solstice was the best chance of the year to get knocked up. It's a real turn-on."

"Lots of March birthdays?" Jen said.

Jacob thought about it. "Yeah, probably."

"I like the dancing around naked part," Maggie said, "but, you're right—I'm not really into the hippie shit that much. No offense though, it works for you."

"None taken. Now come here and let me spank that attitude out of you."

"Nope." Maggie stood up slowly, feeling the complete effects of her high. She was slightly dizzy. "No spankings. No drum circles. No hippies. We have to go meet the guys, I think. How much do we owe you for the bag?"

"On the house," Jacob said. "Boat. On the house-boat. Get it?"

"Hilarious. Are you sure we can't pay you?" Beth said.

"Sure as can be. Maggie, it was great to see you, stay safe out there. Girls, it was good hanging out again."

"Thanks, Jacob," Jen said, hugging him. Beth waved, said thanks, and walked toward their car.

"When will I see you again?" Maggie said, looking down at his bare feet. One of his toes was missing. She wondered why she hadn't noticed at the party when they were lying naked on the bed together—probably because she was drunk at the time.

"That depends on you. When do you want to see me again?"

"Let me get through this weekend, and then I'll give you a call. Have fun at your ancient pagan drum circle hippie-fest."

"Have fun on your teenage sex romp jock cheerleader light beer puke-fest."

"I will," she whispered in his ear, and then licked it. He kissed her fully on the mouth and squeezed her tightly. She walked away backward, looking at him.

Jacob stood still in front of his rusted white microbus until the girls had pulled out of the parking lot and were circling back up the on-ramp. When they were out of sight, he jumped back in the VW, laughing.

"Holy shit," he shouted, grinning ear to ear. "Did you catch all that?" His eyes blazed in the rearview mirror. A pair of tiny black eyes sparkled from under the pile of blankets on the bed in back.

"Yes," a voice croaked. "We did."

5

The boys pulled into Utica half an hour later, half drunk and smiling. A cop car nosed out from behind a bank as they turned onto Main Street, and Scott pumped the breaks. The three turned their heads simultaneously as they cruised past the squad car, and a pie-faced officer glared back at them.

"Well, shit," Jerrod said. The two up front nodded and both held their cans down low. The cop turned out into the street as they passed and followed close behind.

A family of four crossed the street a block ahead, and Scott rolled to a stop. The cop car pulled up on their tail.

"Fucking pedestrians," Jerrod said. The dad and mom crossing in front of the jeep wore pastel golf shirts. The mom had a sweater tied around her neck. The boy stopped in the middle of the street to pick something up. "Jesus Christ, kid!" Jerrod said. "Get the fuck out of the road!"

"Jerrod, shut up," Peter said. "Hand me your beer, I'll put it back in the cooler."

"I'm not done with it yet," Jerrod replied.

"Goddammit, shut the fuck up and hand me your beer!"

"Both of you chill out," Scott said, checking the rearview mirror. "The cop's not gonna do anything. We aren't speeding."

The dad walked back and grabbed his son by the arm.

"Come on," Scott sneered. "That pig should arrest them for jaywalking. What the fuck, man." The dad scowled as he dragged his son across the street, and Scott resumed down the block.

The cop followed until the next light then swerved off to the left.

"Fucking tourists," Peter said. "Just walk out in front of traffic, you dumb shits. Obviously the police don't give a fuck."

"Hey, you guys see a liquor store anywhere?" Jerrod asked.

They looked on both sides of the street as they rolled down the main drag. Harley Davidson motorcycles sat out in a row in front of a local bar. Kids stepped out of an ice cream parlor with tall red, white, and blue ice cream cones. They passed a closed restaurant and a t-shirt shop, but no liquor store. At the end of the next block, they saw a large vinyl sign advertising "wine tastings."

"You think the girls would want some vino?" Peter asked his friends.

"You probably do, you fag," Jerrod replied.

"Mm, yes," Scott chipped in, "my name is Peter. My boyfriend and I would like a peach spritzer."

"Whatever, pull in here," Peter said. "I don't see any liquor store, and I don't feel like driving all over looking for one. I know Maggie likes white wine anyway." As they pulled up, two women in their mid-forties got out of a Cadillac Escalade and walked toward the winery. Peter noticed one in particular who wore a white tank top pulled tight across her chest.

"Fuck yeah, look at that shit," Jerrod said from the back seat. "Two MILFs getting some booze." He stood up and leaned over the roll bar. "Excuse me, ma'am?" The two women turned. One smirked and continued walking, while the tank-topped one walked toward the Jeep.

"You better not stand up in that while you're moving; you might fall out," she said.

"Don't worry about that, I'm a professional," Jerrod said. Scott pulled to a stop, and he and Peter jumped out. "Do you know where a liquor store is around here?" Jerrod asked.

The woman breathed in, showing off her profile as she looked up and down the street. Scott walked into the store, and Peter stood watching as a spectator.

"No. Looks like you already found one though," she said, pointing to the pile of empty cans in the backseat. "You look like you're my son's age. Are you even old enough to drink?"

"I'm old enough for a lot of things," Jerrod said as he leaped out of the backseat. He walked right up to the blond mom. "We've got a houseboat for the weekend. Would you and your friend care to join us?"

The woman stepped back and laughed out loud. "Yeah, right. I'm sure our husbands wouldn't notice us missing for the weekend." She started walking back toward the entrance, and Jerrod and Peter followed.

"Well maybe we'll run into you out on the river," Peter offered. "You're welcome on our boat anytime."

The woman stopped before the door and turned to face them both. "I've been thinking lately that it would be kind of fun to party with a bunch of teenage boys," she said. Peter and Jerrod looked at each other, and then back at her. "My husband works night and day, and I just sit around the house, reading romance novels and thinking crazy thoughts."

Peter swallowed. "What kind of crazy thoughts?" he asked.

The door swung open, and the woman's friend stuck her head out. "Mandy, are you going to sample some wine with me or are not?" She gave the two guys a once-over and then looked back at her friend.

"I'm coming, hold on," Mandy said. "These two young gentlemen have invited us to their houseboat for the weekend. Wouldn't that be nice?"

"No offense, boys, but I don't think you could handle us," the woman said.

"I'd love to find out," Jerrod replied.

Mandy snickered. "All right, enough from you two," she said as she walked inside. "You boys have fun playing with each other."

Peter followed right behind. "We have girls meeting us at the marina."

"Yeah," Jerrod said, "hot young girls who like to fuck."

Mandy turned around and smacked Jerrod across the face. Her friend, five other customers, and the woman behind the tasting counter all stopped what they were doing and stared. "You watch your mouth, you little shit. Why don't you show some respect?"

"Jesus Christ, lady! Why'd you hit me?" Jerrod's face burned red.

"We're sorry." Peter stepped in. "He didn't mean anything."

A man came out from behind a door marked Office. "Is there a problem here, miss?" he asked.

Mandy held her chin up and peered down at Jerrod. "No problem. Just teaching these boys some manners."

"Well, then I suggest you buy something, sample something, or get out," he said.

Mandy walked over to her friend and shrugged. Jerrod rubbed his cheek and looked around.

Peter walked up to the counter and asked for a sample of something red. The girl working gave him a plastic thimble of red wine. He took a drink and thought it tasted like rhubarb. "Too sweet. What do you have that girls would like?"

"A lot," she said.

"What do you recommend?"

"What type of wine does she like?"

"I don't know. White?"

"Can I see your ID?"

"You already served me something."

"ID."

Peter shrugged and pulled out his wallet. He gave her his fake. It was someone else's ID who looked vaguely similar to him. The girl gazed at the ID for a few seconds.

"Where's the birthdate on this?" she asked.

"Top left."

"Okay, here you go," she said as she handed it back. "So what do you want?"

"Your cheapest bottle of white wine." He realized as he stood there that Scott wasn't in the store.

The girl put a bottle down on the counter. Rock River White. "Is this good?"

"It's okay."

"How much do I owe you?"

"Thirty-nine fifty."

"Thirty-nine fifty…what the f…," he muttered. "Never mind."

"Whatever," she said, and put the bottle back up on the shelf.

Peter walked over to Jerrod. "Have you seen Scott?" he asked.

"Did you see the tits on Mandy?" Jerrod replied. "Tell me you wouldn't want to titty-fuck those delicious milkers."

"Of course I would, but where's Scott?"

"How the fuck would I know? He's probably taking a dump. Do you think she'll come over to our boat?"

"To slap you again? Hopefully." Peter saw another exit toward the far end of the store. He walked outside into a large fenced-in yard. Tall trees shaded the grass, and several people sat out in cast iron chairs. Scott was sitting next to Mandy and her friend. Each had a glass of wine in hand.

"Scott," Peter said, "we're going."

Scott casually waved him off, and appeared to be telling some hilarious story to the two older women. They both laughed as he sat back and sipped his drink.

Jerrod walked up behind Peter. "What the fuck! Look at that asshole sitting there. He's putting the moves on my MILFs!"

"Your MILFs? Dude, seriously, let's get the fuck out of here. The wine costs forty fucking dollars a bottle."

"That's some high-class trim right there, buddy. Maggie and her friends have the bodies of ten-year-old boys compared to those two. I've gotta hit that shit." Jerrod walked over to the three seated together. "Ladies, please ignore everything my friend says. He's nineteen, he works in an ice cream factory, and he's a bed wetter."

Scott threw his drink on the grass, lunged out of his chair, and tackled Jerrod across the lawn. The women jumped up and screamed, and the man from inside the winery ran out.

"Get off my property!" he yelled. "I'm calling the cops, break it up!" Jerrod had pinned Scott and was rubbing his face in the grass. Peter grabbed Jerrod by the collar and pulled him up. "All three of you, get lost!"

The boys ran back through the store and out into the front parking lot. Jerrod jumped in back of the Jeep, Scott turned the ignition on, and Peter flipped over the roll bar into the passenger side. His feet slammed down hard on Scott's shoulder.

Scott howled and slugged Peter back. "That's my bad shoulder, you fucking asshole!" he yelled.

Peter looked back and saw the same cop from Main Street flying into the parking lot with lights flashing. "God fucking dammit," he said.

The cop pulled up behind the Jeep. Jerrod kicked the cans under the seats. The three boys turned forward. Scott watched the officer get out and walk toward them in the rearview mirror. The cop carried a clipboard in one hand and kept his other hand down by his gun holster.

"License and registration," he said in a nasally Southern accent. Scott handed him his actual driver's license and registration out of the middle console. The cop looked at the paperwork for several seconds and then jotted something down on the clipboard. "Where you boys from?"

"Dixon," Peter said.

The cop took off his polarized glasses to reveal a pair of dark beady eyes. "Dixon what?" he asked.

"Dixon, Illinois," Scott replied.

The cop leaned his head in so his face was inches from Scott's.

"I know where Dixon is on a map, young man," he growled. "When you answer my questions, you address me as 'sir.'" He leaned back out of the Jeep, and the boys were silent. "Now, one more time. Where. Are. You. Boys. From?"

"Dixon, sir," Peter said.

"You shut up." He pointed at Peter, and then jabbed Scott with the end of his clipboard. "You say it."

"Dixon, sir," Scott said.

"All right then. Tell me this. Do they tolerate 'disturbing the public' in Dixon?"

"No, sir," Scott said. The three kept their heads straight ahead.

"Well then, why do you think we would tolerate it here in the beautiful township of Utica?"

"We weren't—" Jerrod started to say.

"Shut up," the cop said. "Now listen here, the three of you. I do not like punks coming through here and horsing around in our establishments. It's bad for business. Do you understand me?"

"Yep," Jerrod said.

"Yes, what?"

"Yes, sir."

"Good. I've got way too much to deal with today to be putting up with pissants like yourselves. Get to wherever you're getting to and knock off the BS." He looked closely at Jerrod. "You boys been drinking?"

"No, sir," Peter said.

The cop glared at the three of them. "Why are you in Utica?"

"We've got a houseboat for the weekend, sir," Peter said, becoming the unofficial group spokesman.

"Houseboat? Well, let me tell you something else. You boys better not let me catch you drinking out on the water. We're patrolling all weekend, and I'll be watching for you." He paused and then took a step back. "You boys hear about the Davis girl?" He had a strange look on his face.

"No, sir."

"You probably wouldn't. You planning to Jet Ski?"

"No, sir."

"Probably for the best. Last week, Miss Jenny Davis was out on her daddy's Jet Ski about five miles upriver. You want to know what happened?"

Peter and Scott exchanged glances.

"What happened to her?"

"She was decapitated," he said, as his eyes widened.

"What the fuck!" Jerrod said. "Decapitated?"

"Watch your mouth, boy," the cop said. "Decapitated. A crying shame. She was prom queen, you know. Type a girl who wouldn't let any one of you touch her, that's for darn sure. The paper said it was an accident. Fishing line got caught up in some branches and tore right through her neck."

"Why are you telling us?" Peter asked.

"'Cause if you're taking out a houseboat, that's the part of the river you'll be on. And I know it weren't no accident."

"What happened?"

"I'll tell you what happened. Someone strung up that line on purpose. I think someone killed her."

"Why?"

"Why? I don't know why. Jealousy. Sick perversions. I just know that too many accidents happen out on the river. And I think that if you boys know what's good for you, you'll cut out all this funny stuff, or there might be another."

"Another accident?" Jerrod asked.

"You've been warned," the cop said, putting his shades back on. "You boys enjoy your vacation now." He walked back to his car.

Peter turned to his two friends. "You think he's fucking with us?"

"Of course he is. Fucking pig," Scott said.

"Well, good thing we don't have any fucking Jet Skis with us," Jerrod said.

Scott backed the Jeep out of the parking lot, and they headed toward the marina.

6

The black Eagle Talon raced north up the back-country road. The driver downshifted into fourth gear and blew past the truck they were flying up on. He had a thick black mustache and a square jaw. He shifted back to fifth and looked over at the young, dark-haired girl in the passenger seat. She had a small upturned nose, black eyes, and dark brown skin. She looked straight ahead, biting her upper lip. He held the steering wheel with one hand. His large forearm was covered with faded black tattoos. He glanced at the clock on the dash. Los Tigres del Norte played at low volume on the AM dial. The driver sped past another farm truck.

"Don't worry about me," the girl said softly in Spanish.

"I'm not worried," he said, whipping around a slow-moving tractor. "You're ready."

"I'm ready," she repeated. She held her petite hands in her lap and hung her head. She closed her eyes and silently recited her prayer. The driver looked straight ahead, cataloging the road and the oncoming traffic. "You hungry?" he asked.

"No."

"I'm starving. Let's get something in the next town."

"Do we have time?" she asked, opening her eyes. He took his gaze off the road long enough to give her a smile.

"Yeah," he said. "I'm hungry. Let's get a burger."

"I don't think they serve burgers this early."

"Yeah, they do," he said. "Everyone serves everything these days."

7

The Jeep passed through the rest of the town. The tourist shops and restaurants gave way to lush green trees and bushes as they came up on a long bridge. As they crossed over, Peter looked down at the dam on the right. A massive barge waited in the lock, and several fishing boats dotted the dark brown river. On the other side, tall cliffs grew up from the banks, and he could see a couple people water-skiing behind the wake of a speedboat.

"They better watch out for fishing line," Peter said out loud.

"I don't feel so hot," Scott answered.

Peter noticed Scott's face looked slightly green. "What's wrong with you? Can't hold your liquor?"

"I think it was whatever I was drinking at that winery," Scott said. "Some fruit shit."

"That's what you get," Jerrod said. "Have a beer."

"No way," Scott shook his head. "You bring any Gatorade?"

"Nope. Just beer and whiskey." Peter looked in the cooler. "I bet the girls brought some." They crossed over to the other side and saw a large billboard on the right for Mac's Marina. "Here we are, gents." They pulled in through an opening between a tall chain link fence, passing rows of gleaming yachts up on hoists.

"I bet those cost a fortune," Jerrod said as he looked up. "Hey, Scott, I could go for a couple fried egg sandwiches right now. How about you?"

"Shut up, man. Seriously. I think I'm gonna puke."

"Some hot greasy mayonnaise and egg sandwiches would be good, with some thick meaty gravy."

Scott pulled up fast to the marina building, put the Jeep in park, leaned out his side, and threw up with an urgent heave.

"What's up, kittens?" Jerrod said to Maggie and Jen, who were standing next to the Sunbird. Jen was eating a bag of puffy Cheetos.

Scott looked up and wiped some vomit off his chin. He forced a smile.

"Fuck you, Jerrod," Jen said. "What took you assholes so long?"

"Hi to you too," Peter said, getting out. "Hey, Maggie, how long have you been waiting?"

"Not long," she shrugged. "What's wrong with him?" Peter walked around the front of the Jeep to Maggie and kissed her. She pulled back. "Oh God, you wreak of beer."

"You wreak of pot."

"Wake-n' bake," Maggie said.

"Couldn't wait for me?"

"Doesn't look like you wasted any time. Least we aren't already puking."

"Scott's the only one who's having trouble holding his liquor."

"I'm fine," Scott said. "Why did you make me drink that shitty-ass wine? You girls bring any Gatorade?"

Maggie rolled her eyes and leaned into the backseat of her car. Peter looked at her ass in her Umbros, her black thong showed as she hunched over. He noticed Jerrod and Scott were watching as well. She stood back up with three bottles of lemon lime. "Here you go." She handed the first one to Scott and smiled. "Beth's holding our place in line. There's like a hundred people here waiting to get their boats."

As the group walked toward the entrance, an obese man flew up in a golf cart. He gripped the wheel with one hand and held a Big Gulp in the other. "You can't park here," he said. Sweat covered his forehead. His flab spilled out from under his shirt and over the side of the cart.

"We're just checking in," Peter said. "We'll move in a second."

"No parking. Can't you see the sign?" he said.

"They're parked here." Peter pointed at the Sunbird. Maggie slugged him.

The man nodded at Maggie and Jen. "They're fine. You're not. Move, or I'll have you towed."

"Jesus Christ. All right," Peter said. Scott tossed the keys to Peter and went inside. "Thanks," Peter said to the fat man. "Where should I park?"

The guy took a drink out of his Big Gulp. "Not here."

Peter drove down a long row of cars and trucks and parked on the end. As he was walking back, the Escalade from the winery pulled in. He waved, and the two women ignored him.

Inside the marina, there were fifteen people standing around. The jaywalker family was at the front of the line, and the dad was arguing with a marina employee behind the counter who looked about twelve. The boy and girl were circling their mother, pinching each other on the arm.

"We reserved the Admiral. We want the Admiral," the dad said.

"I understand, sir, but the Admiral is out of commission. The Captains are what we have, and they're just as good." The wife with the sweater sighed.

"Typical. We want to speak to the person in charge. We didn't come all the way out here to get screwed over," she said, and then turned to her kids. "Would you two cut it out?" The kids giggled and kept at it.

"Honey, easy," the husband said, rubbing her back. "We want to talk with the manager."

"Great," Jerrod said. "You've been here an hour, you couldn't have the boat ready for us?"

"Fuck you, Jerrod," Beth said. "They won't let us take it out until we're all here."

Peter said, "Hi," to Beth, and saw that Scott was looking better.

"Well, we're all here now," Scott said. "Can't we get going?"

"We're after these guys," Beth said, pointing to the two middle-aged men in front of them. Peter glanced back at Maggie and then turned back to the family at the counter.

"Mom!" The girl pulled on her mother's arm. "Bobby pinched me real hard."

"Robert, don't pinch your sister."

"But she pinched me first," Robert whined.

The mother grabbed him by the arm to hold him still. "I said, don't pinch your sister—got it?"

"Robert, don't pinch your sister. Go look at that stuff over there," the father said. "If you're good, I'll buy you something."

"Uh! How come Bobby gets something, and I don't get anything? It's not fair!" the girl said, crossing her arms.

"I'll get you each something. Just behave, or we won't get a boat at all, and you can do chores all weekend instead," he said. The girl ran off to join her brother who was busy pulling t-shirts down off a rack.

"Good morning, ma'am, what can I do you for?" A booming voice came from the back of the room.

Every eye in the marina, except the two kids', turned to look at the source of the voice. A man walked up behind the counter. His head was square, his chin jutted out from his weatherworn face like a lunch box. Short white hair stuck out from a sailor cap with a golden anchor on the front. His eyes were blue, making his sunburned skin look even darker. He looked old and tough. He towered over the husband and wife.

"Welcome to Mac's. I'm Bill. What seems to be the trouble?"

"No trouble," the husband said nervously. "We reserved a houseboat, and your employee told us it's unavailable."

"The Queen Mary's out of commission, it's true." He hung his head. "Some idiot pulled up onto a log just yesterday. Tore a nasty hole right through the hull. Tell you what though, ma'am, we've got a whole fleet of houseboats for you that will fit you and your kids just fine. Now if I can have a credit card and ID, I'll get you set up right away."

A deafening blast of noise throttled the room. Everyone except Bill jumped.

"You use it, you buy it," Bill said to little Robert, who was holding a boat horn in one hand and wearing a look of shock on his face.

"Goddammit, Robert! What did I tell you?" the dad shouted. Robert placed the horn back on the shelf and ran outside crying. The girl started crying and ran out to follow him.

"Jesus Christ, can we get this show on the road?" Jerrod muttered.

The husband shrugged, told the wife to go get the kids, and gave his card to the man. Peter watched the transaction and felt himself sobering up. The door opened, and Mandy and her friend walked in.

"Nice," Jerrod said. Mandy glanced at the group and then walked up to one of the two middle aged men ahead of Beth. "Oh," Jerrod muttered under his breath. "Great. I think I'll go outside for some air." Scott agreed, and they both quickly exited.

"What's up with those two?" Jen asked.

"They're preparing for an ass kicking," Peter said, watching Mandy talk to the two men. He couldn't hear what she was saying.

Maggie watched the women also, and looked out a window to see Jerrod peaking in. "What did you guys do?"

"I didn't do anything," Peter said.

A minute went by, and the two men didn't run out, so he relaxed a little. Maggie stuck a piece of gum in her mouth and started smacking. Half an hour later, they finally stepped up to the counter.

"Welcome to Mac's Marina. What can I do you for?" the man addressed Maggie and Peter.

"Are you Mac?" Peter asked.

"No, I'm Bill," Bill said.

"Who's Mac?" Peter asked. Maggie pinched his side.

"Who's Mac?" Bill laughed. "Field Marshal Douglas Macarthur." He pointed to a photo up on the wall of some military brass wading up the shore of the Philippines. "You kids don't read your history anymore, do you? Well, Mac's the man in charge, the rest of us can only aspire." He gazed up at the photo for a moment and then turned back toward Peter. "Lost my big toe in doubleyah doubleyah two. Some sneaky Jap was hiding in one of those mountain foxholes, caught me off guard." He paused. "Look at me carrying on, though. Renting a houseboat? You need to be twenty-five to rent a boat from me."

"No problem, I'm twenty-six," Maggie said, handing him a fake. "My mom called down with the credit card number a week ago." Bill looked at the ID and then took it in back to make a copy. Maggie glanced at Peter.

"I can't believe you talked me into this. What if I get caught?"

"Shh, you're fine," Peter said.

Bill walked back, beaming. "Yep, got your number, here's your DL, young lady. How many in your party?"

"Six," Maggie said.

"Any of you ever pilot a houseboat before?" Bill asked.

"I've had a boating license since I was fourteen," Peter said. "Both my friends grew up around boats."

"My dad used to take us out on a houseboat on Lake Powell every year." Maggie paused then added, "Until he died."

"I'm sorry to hear that, young lady. Sounds like you're qualified, so just sign these waivers." He handed her several forms to fill out. She signed her name to match the name on the fake and handed them back. Bill folded the documents up and shoved them below the counter. "Now, you get your party together, and I'll meet you down by slip number thirteen in about fifteen minutes."

The two walked away from the counter, but halfway to the door, Peter turned around. "Can I ask you something, Bill?"

"Shoot," Bill said.

"Is it true that a girl died around here last week?" Peter asked, walking back up to the counter.

Bill bowed his head and sighed, "Jennifer Davis. What a tragic accident. Yes, it's true."

"She was decapitated?"

"Shh," Bill exclaimed, looking around at the other people who had filed in. "Ixnay on the ecapitay, if you know what I mean." He craned his neck past Peter and addressed the others. "Be right with you folks." Then he leaned in close, and Peter followed. "Look kid, accidents happen all the time out on the river. Folks come out here from the city, don't know how to swim, don't know how to pilot a seafaring vessel. Things happen. Total freak accident, getting caught up in fishing line like that."

"Some cop in town told us it wasn't an accident."

"Not an accident? Shoot. Bet that was Tim. Probably trying to keep you on your toes. No, son, that poor girl was just plain unlucky. In a million years, I've never heard of anyone else getting killed from a fishing line. You'd have a better chance of your boat getting struck by lightning and frying to death, and that ain't never happened around here neither."

"All right, thanks. We'll meet you out by the boat then?"

"Lucky slip thirteen," he said in a louder tone. "Gather up your friends, and I'll see you in a jiffy. Oh and, son, let's keep that story to ourselves, shall we?"

8

The group pulled both cars around next to a line of houseboats tied off to a long dock made of wooden planks. The boats all looked the same: wide, white, flat on top. Jerrod hopped down onto the bow of theirs in slip number thirteen and walked into the cabin. The girls started pulling plastic bags of groceries out of the Pontiac.

Peter took his backpack out of the Jeep and stepped down into the boat. The platform shifted under his weight. He walked into the cabin and looked around. To his right, an L-shaped couch covered with old striped fabric. On his left, the steering wheel in front of a panel of instruments. A CB radio sat next to a book of maps. Behind the captain's chair, a wooden cabinet held a small TV, a DVD player, and a space for food. As he walked back, he took inventory of the sink, the old metal refrigerator, a tiny bathroom, and a card table surrounded by another couch. A narrow corridor led to the back, and on either side were two small, dark bedrooms separated from the main cabin by thin curtains. He stuck his head in the grungy bathroom, looked at the shower, then walked out onto the stern. A large square with a plywood cover dominated the platform, with just enough space to walk around to a spiral ladder leading to the roof. He leaned over the back to look at the muddy water.

With a blood curdling scream and a crash, the water exploded into his face, drenching his head and shirt. He jumped back and shouted, looking up and around to see what had just happened.

Jerrod shot out of the water and laughed. "You pussy!"

"Dude, what the fuck!" Peter said, pushing his wet bangs out of his eyes.

"Check it out! Waterslide!" Jerrod said, pointing up toward the right side of the boat.

Peter looked over to see. Sure enough, there was a waterslide extending from the top of the boat to about four feet over the water. "We haven't even left the marina yet, douchebag. Why don't you help with the unpacking?" Peter said. He heard a woman laughing and looked over to see Mandy standing in back of the houseboat next to them. Jerrod laughed and waved.

"That's pretty stupid to jump into the water here. It's too shallow," she said.

"Thanks, mom!" Jerrod said. "The water's great, you should join me!" As he finished, Mandy's husband walked up behind Mandy and looked at the two boys.

"This is my husband, Joe," she said, turning to greet him. "These are the two I told you about from Rock River Vineyards."

"You guys aren't going to be blaring your music tonight on the river are you?" Joe asked with an edge to his voice.

Jerrod pulled himself up by a metal ladder hanging off the back of the boat. Peter began to shake his head no, when the first notes of "Baby Got Back" came blasting out of the cabin. He turned to see Beth and Jen dancing in the kitchen area while Scott was opening a case of beer.

"We'll stay clear of you guys. It's a big river," Peter said.

"I hope so. We definitely don't want to listen to that shit all weekend."

"No problem," Peter said, and followed Jerrod back inside the boat.

"Prick," Jerrod said.

"Fucknut," Peter said.

"Stupid fucking asshole Viagra motherfucker. I'm gonna fuck his wife tonight. You just watch."

"Tonight, huh? Joe seems to be an open-minded guy. He's probably down."

They both grabbed a beer and started unpacking the food.

"All right, people. Turn that garbage off for two seconds." Bill's voice came from the dock. "If you don't want to get stuck out on the river with a dead engine, and you don't want your toilet backing up, and you don't want to tear up this rig on some driftwood, then I need your undivided attention." He stepped onto the bow with the manner of a drill sergeant and proceeded to rattle off a list of instructions that made the party's eyes roll back in their heads.

Peter tried to pay attention, but after ten minutes of "press this button to raise the trim," and "flip this switch to turn the fog lights on," he saw that Scott was following pretty closely and decided he could sit down on the couch and tune out.

"This is important." Bill looked right at Peter. "Come over here, all of you." They huddled around the book of maps he held up. "Downstream is the dam, so you won't get very far that way. You can go through the lock, but I don't recommend it unless you want to kill three hours waiting between the barges. Speaking of barges, don't get anywhere near them. Even in a boat this size, you get too close, and you might end up getting run over. Now, look here." He pointed at some islands on the map with his middle finger. "Tonight, you can pull up on this island here, or you can stay on the shore up here, but stay away from that island." He looked at Beth, then Jen, then Maggie, and then back at the map. "This island is surrounded by some old concrete blocks that will tear the bottom right out from under you. The others are okay. But don't go walking too far in. They're covered in poison ivy."

"Why concrete blocks?" Jen asked.

Bill smiled and batted his eyelashes at her several times before answering, "Old construction projects. They used to mine some of these islands decades ago."

"Mine those islands? They look tiny."

"Don't ask me. They were digging for King Solomon's gold, for all I know. What I do know is: if you plan on getting your deposit back in full, this boat's got to come back in as good of shape as when you took it out. Do not—I repeat—do not go near this island."

"Got it," Peter said. "Don't go near that island. Anything else?"

Bill squinted. "Yes, anything else. We're just getting started. Now, on to the living room area." He shut the book of maps and took one step backward. "Here you have your TV. It's not HD. It's not widescreen. It's not dish. It's not cable. It's regular old antenna television. Gets in one channel. Local. Only thing on this time of day is the gospel shows." He looked at Jerrod, still sopping wet in his clothes. "Everyone needs a little JC," he said in all seriousness. "Looks like you boys could use all you can get."

After a few minutes, Bill finally made his way to the engine under the plywood canopy in back. The engine casing was massive. Bill held up his middle finger several times to demonstrate where to push or prod if, for whatever reason, the engine stopped working. When he finally finished, he dropped the lid back down, took off his hat to reveal his short, white buzz cut, looked each of the group in the eye, and said, "Any questions?" Peter looked down to see that his big toe was in fact missing from his left foot. "Richard here's going to tow you out of the marina. Then you're on your own. Call me on channel five of the CB if anything comes up. Otherwise, stay safe and bring her back in one piece." Bill paused for a few seconds then pulled his cap back on and marched off the boat.

9

Richard, who turned out to be the fat guy from the marina parking lot, had exchanged his golf cart for a johnboat. He tossed a line to their houseboat and then tugged them out to the open water. Once they were in the current, Scott turned on the engine, checked a few gauges, and then steered them slowly across the river to the far side.

Jen and Maggie went into one of the bedrooms and came back out a few minutes later in bikinis. Beth pulled her jean shorts off to reveal a pair of black bottoms to match her top. Peter whistled. Scott took his eye off the water to watch the three as they paraded down the back and up the ladder. Jerrod handed the two guys a cold beer each and cracked one open for himself. Peter exchanged Beth's mix CD for a live Social Distortion disc in the DVD player, and the noise of cheering faded up out of the TV speakers.

"Well boys..." Peter held up his beer. "Here's to getting laid on the motherfucking houseboat!"

The three raised their cans together and then chugged. Three empties were tossed on the ground, and three more were opened. Peter sat back on the couch and watched the sandstone cliffs high above them. He saw a bird hovering above the treetops but couldn't tell if it was an eagle or a vulture. Another houseboat was chugging along about a half mile upstream. He guessed it was probably the jaywalkers. Another boat was pulling out of the marina behind them. He could see Mandy and her friend up on the roof.

"Hey, did either of you guys bring binoculars?" Peter asked.

"What do you see?" Scott asked, looking ahead.

"I think our friends from the winery are topless." All three whipped around and strained to get a look.

"Holy shit, I think they are. Look at that shit!" Jerrod said. "I knew it! That Mandy wants to faugh-uk!"

"I wonder if we can get our chicks to go topless," Scott said.

The three looked at each other, and then Jerrod shot toward the ladder. Peter raised his eyebrow to Scott and then raced after.

"Hey, you assholes, don't leave me down here by myself!"

"You're the captain, man. Don't run into anything," Peter shouted as he climbed the ladder. The three girls were lounging on deck chairs, wearing both their tops and their bottoms.

"Maggie, you see that boat over there." Jerrod pointed. "You three should flash them."

Maggie sat up, pulled down her sunglasses to look and then put them back on and lay back. "You wish. I'm way too sober."

"I think you look great in your bikini," Peter said to Maggie.

Jen and Beth looked at each other and smirked.

"I think that bikini would look better floating in the river," Jerrod said. "Which one of you wants to jump off the slide with me?"

"You can't go down the slide with the engine on," Jen said. "The propeller will cut your dick off."

Jerrod laughed.

Peter looked back at Mandy again and then surveyed both sides of the river. "This is beautiful—out here with all the trees and the sunshine and shit," he said. "I'm going back down for another beer. Anyone want anything?"

"Can you bring up those Coronas?" Beth asked.

Peter nodded and left Jerrod up with the girls. He brought back the bottles, a lime, and a small knife, and then climbed back down the ladder again to join Scott.

Scott was reading the map and looking to match landmarks on the river. "I think we're about five miles from the first island. I'm not sure how long it will take to get up there," he said.

"It's only two. We have all the time in the world," Peter said, sitting back on the couch. "Good to be back here with you, man."

"Same here, Pete. You're lucky you got out. It's boring as shit in D-town."

"You can come visit anytime. You've always got a place to crash in Colorado."

"Thanks, man. I might take you up on that one of these days."

Peter watched the sunlight sparkle on the water. Scott held the wheel and looked at the map. The two listened to the live version of "Bad Luck" playing through the TV.

10

In the late afternoon, they pulled the boat onto a sandbar on the south side of the river, where Bill had recommended. The water was shallow, allowing them to wade back and forth with ease. Peter tied the anchor line around a large tree and then started hauling food, beer, and tents with the rest of the group. Their campsite was pristine. Between thick patches of trees and bushes, an opening of soft green grass spread out at the foot of a sandstone cliff. The cliff face, at least one hundred feet up, was pocked with holes, where tiny birds flew in and out of their nests. Beth and Jen worked together to put up their tent. Scott had a large summer tent he set up right against the cliff, and Jerrod gathered dead branches for firewood.

Peter set up his two-man tent a little farther away from the group, threw his backpack into the tent, and then strung a camping hammock between the cotton trees. White cottonseeds drifted down through the hot muggy air, and some stuck to the sweat of his skin.

When he finished the hammock, he gave it a try, swinging gently with one leg on the ground and looking up at the lush treetops and the cliff soaring above. He looked over and watched Maggie talking with Jen and Beth.

"Maggie, come over here for a second," he called.

"Give me a minute," she said, and waved.

He looked at her thin arms in her tank top and the line of her neck. Jerrod waded out to the boat, disappeared into the cabin, and then came back out with a football. He hurled it toward Scott. Scott took a running start for the water and dove in to make the catch. The girls cheered.

"Come on, Peter, let's play!" Scott yelled.

Peter glanced at Maggie, then pulled himself up out of the hammock and splashed into the water. The water was cool. He caught the ball and threw back to Jerrod. The girls all stripped down to their bikinis and joined the guys out on the sandbar. The sun blazed down on them, without a cloud in the sky. After a few minutes of catch, they formed teams. One end zone was the shore, and the other, the boat. Jerrod threw a spiral to Maggie, who caught it and ran toward the shore, and Scott tackled her into the water. She came up laughing hysterically. After a few missed catches, Peter had the ball and was high-stepping toward the boat. He tried to lunge past Beth, but she reached out and grabbed on to his bathing suit. She yanked it down around his legs and then crashed into him as he fell into the river.

"Hey, personal foul!" he yelled, gulping water. He reached out to grab her top, but she pulled away too quickly.

"Whew! Naked man!" Beth yelled, pointing.

The game came to an end as everyone laughed. Peter pulled his shorts back up and slogged his way back to the beach. "Who's ready for a beer?" he asked as he got one for himself out of the cooler. The group joined him, drinking cold beer out of cans as they sat on the grass.

"What a beautiful day," Maggie said. "It's so nice to get away from it all."

Jerrod pulled up the grass where he sat. Scott swatted a mosquito on his neck.

"Anyone want to get high?" Jen said, pulling a thin joint from her backpack.

"Does the pope shit in the woods?" Scott said. "Fuck, yeah."

Jen lit up and coughed. "This is the kibby kibby," she said, and passed it to Scott.

Scott took a drag and hacked. "Holy crap, that's harsh. Where'd you score this shit?"

"It's Magg's," Jen said. "You're just used to smoking that ditch weed. This is the good stuff."

"Well, all right Maggie," Jerrod said. "Since when do you have the hookup?"

"I've got my connections," Maggie said, glancing at Beth, and then took a drag. She held it in and then exhaled slowly. She passed the joint to Peter.

After a puff, he lay back with his head against Maggie's leg and stared up at the sky. A solitary cloud floated by overhead. Peter felt the sweat drip off his underarms and felt the heat of Maggie's thigh against his neck. A dull pressure grew under his eyes, and after a few minutes, he felt sort of dizzy. When it came around again, Maggie held it up to his lips, and he took another drag.

"Do you guys know what tomorrow is?" Jen asked, playing with her dirty blond dreads.

"The twenty-first?" Peter said.

"Do you know what holiday it is?" Jen asked.

"Are you going to tell us?" Jerrod said.

"None of you boys know? We all know," she said. "Summer solstice."

"We should celebrate," Beth said. "Who's going to be the summer solstice queen?"

"Peter," Jerrod said. "The summer solstice queen."

"Fuck you," Peter said, still looking up in the air. "What's summer solstice?"

"Well, Peter," Jen giggled, "let me tell you. Before they had Christmas, or Easter, the ancients would celebrate the longest days and shortest days of the year."

"Like Stonehenge shit?"

"Yeah, like druids and pagans, you know. They would make sacrifices and offerings to their gods to ensure the fertility of their crops."

"You mean, like crops," Scott said, waving the joint.

"You mean, like your fertile valley?" Jerrod said to Beth.

"You know the maypole?" Jen said. "When they have the little grade school kids parade around the flagpole with ribbons? That's totally a pagan ritual. It's actually a phallus."

"Phallus!" Jerrod yelled. "I've got your maypole right here."

"Well, Jen," Peter said, "does this mean we have to sacrifice something in order to keep this sweet weed in abundance?"

"Someone," Beth said. "Human sacrifice was a part of the rituals."

"Sounds good," Scott said. "I call, 'Not it.'"

"Not it!" the rest of the group rang out.

"I guess we'll have to find a virgin somewhere by Saturday, so we can do it up right," Peter said.

"Won't find any here," Beth said.

Maggie glanced at Jen but didn't get any reaction.

"Jerrod, you're a virgin, aren't you?" Scott said. Jerrod punched him hard in the arm.

"Fuck no, bro," Jerrod said. "Your mom took care of that back when I was in grade school, bitch."

"Looks like we've got some company," Jen said. She pointed downriver.

11

Coming toward them was a little fishing boat. They watched it approach. Peter could see two people: a man and a kid, maybe a little girl. They watched as the boat pulled up until it was about thirty feet from the houseboat, then the man cut the engine and tossed over an anchor. Beth finished off the joint and crushed out the remains.

"Great," Scott said. "The whole goddamn river and they have to pull up here."

"Who cares?" Maggie said. "It looks like they're just fishing."

The man did in fact have a fishing pole out. He cast the line downstream then handed it to the kid. He cast out a second line, and then the two sat there, staring out into the water.

"Maybe if we crank some tunes, they'll leave us alone," Jerrod said. "What do you think—NWA?"

"Honestly, they're fine. Leave them be," Maggie said.

Jerrod glared at them from behind his beer. He finished it, tossed the empty can by the fire pit, and then stood up. "No, this is our spot, we got here first." He walked down to the water's edge. "Hey, you!" The guy in the boat ignored him. "Hey, you! Take off! This is our campsite!" He waded a few feet into the river. "Hey, can't you hear me? I said get out of here!" The fisherman turned his head, looked at Jerrod, and then turned back. "I said get the fuck out of here, asshole!"

The man on the boat reeled in his line and set the pole down in the boat. He cupped his hands around his mouth and shouted back, "Quiet man, you'll scare the fishes!"

Jerrod laughed and kicked the water. "I said go fish somewhere else!"

"Be quiet, man. I'm just trying to do some fishing with my daughter. I don't want any trouble."

Jerrod shook his head and ran back up on shore. Peter watched the man on the boat cast his line back in. A moment later a small log flew overhead and landed with a large splash, inches from the boat.

"Leave, asshole!" Jerrod stood with another piece of dead log in hand, ready to throw. The man pulled up their anchor, turned the outboard engine on, and started trolling closer to shore.

"You shouldn't have thrown that," the man shouted over the engine. As they approached, Peter could see he looked Mexican, as did his daughter. "You could have hit my girl."

Jerrod held up the log. "Then go, before I have you deported!"

"Jerrod, Jesus," Beth said, standing up. "Sorry!"

The boat sailed up onto the sandbar. The man cut the engine and hopped over the side. The girl stayed on the boat. Jerrod rushed up to meet him. The man was stocky, with a wide face and a thick mustache. He waded up to face Jerrod. Standing toe to toe, Jerrod was a good five inches taller. Jerrod lifted his wooden weapon, but the man didn't flinch.

"Fuck off, beaner." Jerrod's voice shook.

In one fluid motion, the man grabbed Jerrod's wrist, pivoted 180 degrees, and flipped him over his shoulder. Jerrod landed hard on his back. The man pinned him down with his knee on his chest.

"You could have hurt my daughter," the man said. "That is not acceptable behavior."

"Get the fuck off me!"

"Neither is your language." He twisted his knee hard down on Jerrod.

"Get off him!" Jen yelled. "Are you guys going to just stand there? Do something."

Peter looked at Scott. Scott walked up. "Hey man, leave him alone. We're sorry."

The man stood up and addressed the group, "My daughter and I have a right to fish here, just like anyone else on this river. I recommend you let us be." He kept an eye on Jerrod, who managed to pull himself up. "No more throwing branches, okay?" He stood watching the group for another moment, then sneered and turned back to his boat. The little black-haired girl watched her dad wade back up and then helped him in. When he situated himself in the boat, he said, "You should be careful."

"Is that a threat?" Peter asked.

"Friendly warning. When it gets dark out, things go bump in the night, you know?" He smiled. "I'm sure your sticks will protect you." He pulled the cord to start the engine, trolled in reverse to deeper water, and then opened the throttle and headed upstream.

Peter could see him converse with his daughter but couldn't hear him.

"Way to go, Jerrod," Jen said. "You actually called him 'beaner'?"

"Oh, now I'm the asshole?" he said. "The guy attacked me!"

"Shut up. You're fine, right?" Scott asked. "Who cares, he's gone now."

"He threatened us. You all heard him. He's going to come back tonight and—"

"And what? He's with his daughter. He's not going to do anything."

"Do you think he saw us smoking up?" Jen asked.

Jerrod laughed.

"If he did, he's not going to say anything," Maggie said. "Jerrod, you threw a fucking log at his daughter. You're lucky you didn't get it any worse than you got. The guy just wants to fish, like he said. Now he's gone. So let's all take a deep breath, drink a beer, start the fire, and just chill."

Jerrod walked away from the group into the trees. Scott handed Peter a cold one.

"Did you see that guy? Holy shit!" Peter said. "That was like kung fu or some shit."

"Yeah, that was awesome," Scott snickered. He held up his can. Peter lifted his and realized his buzz was gone.

Jerrod re-emerged with a long branch and started picking off the shoots.

"Dude, the guy's gone," Peter said. "You don't have to throw any more branches."

"I'm not going to throw anything," Jerrod said. "When Paco comes back, I'm going to shove this right up his Mexican ass."

"Unless he kicks your ass again first," Maggie said.

Jerrod sat down Indian-style next to them, pulled out a Swiss army knife, and started whittling.

"Well, hurray for the Boy Scouts," Peter said. "Watch out for the scout master."

Jerrod didn't respond but kept shaving the branch to make a spear. Jen and Maggie made eye contact, rolled their eyes, and Beth tried to hold in a laugh.

"Well, what an exciting afternoon. I'm going to get some bug spray," she said, swatting her shoulder. "Need anything from the tent?" she asked, looking at Maggie and then at Jen. Peter watched Maggie and then realized Maggie's things were in the girls' tent.

"All three of you staying in that one tent?" he asked. The three girls smiled and nodded. "That's going to be pretty cramped," he said, addressing Maggie. "I've got plenty of room in mine, if you want."

"Oh, I don't know," she said, standing up and brushing off her bottom. "We'll have to see how the night goes."

"Yeah, Peter," Jen said, "all three of us, so hot in that little tent, wearing next to nothing."

Jerrod stopped carving for a moment, staring at Jen with his mouth open. Peter and Scott looked at each other with raised eyebrows.

"You two staying in Scott's tent?" Peter asked Jerrod and Scott.

"I'm not sleeping tonight. I'm going to be waiting for fucknut," Jerrod said, back to his carving.

Scott started to put some twigs and small branches in the fire pit. Peter finished his beer, got another out of the cooler, and then watched Scott start the fire. When the flame started to catch, he helped Scott lean some bigger logs over the kindling, and soon a strong red fire cracked in the middle of the pit.

"So which of the sisters are you going for?" Peter asked Scott.

"I don't know, man. They're both pretty hot, huh?"

Peter nodded his head in agreement.

"I think we need to divide and conquer, my friends," Peter said. "Jerrod, you like Jen, right? You go after her. Scott, you take Beth. And then I'll get some time with Maggie. Maybe I'll take her out on the boat."

"The boat! I'll take the boat. With Beth," Jerrod said.

"Fine, the boat. Scott, you good with Jen?"

"What, are we taking dibs on the women? You heard them. They're all staying in their tent together. How'd you like to be a fly on the wall for that?"

"I'd like to have my fly down for that," Peter said. "Come on guys, seriously. I need some alone time with Maggie. I haven't spent hardly any time with her since I've been back."

"What are we having for dinner?" Beth said, all of a sudden standing with them.

"We've got some brats and some dogs," Scott said.

Beth walked over and snatched the spear out of Jerrod's hands.

"Thanks for the weenie roaster, J," she said, holding the pointed end out at Scott. "Brat me up, Scotty."

12

As the sun fell behind the treetops, the air cooled off but held on to the humidity. They ate hotdogs and baked beans out of a can, and passed around a bag of potato chips. Jen and Beth and Maggie drank bottles of Corona, and the boys drank cans of Coors Light. The empties were tossed into the fire, and every half hour Scott or Peter would add another log. Jerrod stoked the flames with his branch.

"Do you know any ghost stories?" Beth asked.

"What about the one where the car keeps tailing the woman, and there's a murderer in the backseat of her car?" Jen said.

"What about the one where the guy keeps hearing, 'Don't roll over, or we'll all die'?" Peter offered.

"You mean the one where the ants are all on a floating turd?" Jerrod said. "That's a classic."

"What about the one where the family moves into the house and it's on an Indian burial ground, and the wife and kids all get murdered by the dad?"

"No, they escape at the end, but the dad gets caught in the house, and it burns to the ground," Jen said. Maggie hung her head. "Oh, sorry Maggie. I'm sorry."

"Don't worry about it. It's nothing."

"How long has it been now?" Jerrod asked.

"Jerrod," Beth said. "Don't be rude."

"No, it's okay," Maggie said. "Two years this September."

"You and your mom must be so strong," Beth said.

"And you were the one who found your dad? What was that like?" Jerrod asked.

Maggie's eyes welled up with tears. "Oh, it was great."

"We can change the subject," Peter said.

"No, it's okay," Maggie sniffled. "It was terrifying. Mom was at the hospital on the nightshift. I came home from cheer practice, I remember, wearing my purple-and-white outfit with the bunched-up sleeves. Daddy's Audi was in the driveway, but no lights were on in the house when I came in. I called out for him a few times. After I didn't get a reply, I thought maybe he was asleep.

"It was only seven or eight when you got home, right?" Jen said.

"Yeah, actually it was seven eleven exactly, because I remember noticing the time in my car. Anyway, I thought maybe he was asleep, or he had walked out somewhere, and that I was alone. So I went upstairs to take a shower." She was silent for a period of time. They all knew the story. The whole town had talked about it for weeks. It even made the cover of the newspaper one day. The flames of the campfire leaped in the dark.

"So when I got out of the shower," Maggie continued, "I heard a noise downstairs, like a shout." I called out to Dad, but still nothing. I started to run downstairs in my towel—not even thinking someone besides Dad might be there. The front door was wide open."

"Oh my God, Maggie," Jen said.

"I shut the door, locked it, and went into the kitchen to call the cops. There he was," she said. "On his back, in a pool of his own blood, his neck cut all the way across."

"Jesus Christ. And wasn't there a note?" Jerrod leaned in.

"Yeah, the note. Stuffed into his mouth."

"Fuck me. What did it say again?"

"Fingerling potatoes."

"Jesus," Scott said, staring at the fire.

"Yeah, that fucking note," Maggie said. "I haven't been able to eat a single French fry ever since."

"And the cops never found the guy who did it?"

"Nope," Maggie said, then inhaled and arched her back. "Mom thinks it's the mob, even though no one knows what the potato reference was all about. Irish mob maybe. Mafia would make sense. Dad couldn't afford the trips he took us on, the house, the pool. I figured his work at the shop was paying the bills. I guess he got in over his head or owed someone too much. The cops say they are still looking, but Mom thinks they're in on it."

"You ever think about trying to find the guy and hunt him down yourself?" Beth asked.

"Every day." She lit up a cigarette. Jerrod nodded for one, and she tossed him her pack. "I miss him so much. I picture Mom staring out the window above the sink, crying every night. She was vacant for months. You two were such good friends to me," she said, looking at Beth and Jen. "There isn't a day that goes by that I don't think about what I could have done differently."

"There's nothing you could have done," Jen said.

"Yeah, there is. I could have looked around the house more. I could have grabbed a kitchen knife and stabbed that guy. If I wasn't a cheerleader, I could have come home early, and Dad would have taken me out to dinner."

"Wow, okay," Peter said. "That sucks, Maggie. I hope they find the killer someday."

"Yeah, Pete, me too," Maggie said. "It's good to talk about it, it's been awhile. We're here to party though, right? Let's not think about death anymore this weekend."

"Did you hear the one about the girl who got her head cut off when she was Jet Skiing?"

"Jesus Christ, Jerrod!" Jen said.

"Oh for fuck's sake," Scott said.

"What? It happened, like right here, didn't it?"

"What are you talking about?" Maggie said.

"Shut up, Jerrod," Peter said.

"No, what?"

"You didn't hear—about the girl who just got her head cut off, on this river, just like a week ago?"

"Jesus, no. You did? Why didn't you tell us?"

"We just heard it back in town. Weird ass cop was telling us."

"Why didn't you say anything," Jen said. "Jesus, I wouldn't have come out here if—"

"Enough," Maggie cut her off. "Enough, enough, enough of the bullshit. What did I say? No more death."

"Fine, sorry." Jerrod said.

The friends fell silent. The fire crackled, casting their shadows high up on the cliff face. The group of friends watched the fire dance, drinking beer and smoking cigarettes. Scott tossed his empty can into the fire. He gazed at the white embers deep in the heart of the fire.

"Let's play Truth or Dare," Beth said, breaking the silence.

"Finally," Jerrod said. "Yes. You go first. Truth or dare?"

"Dare," she said. "But nothing stupid."

"Hey, you wanted to play. Okay, dare...dare. I dare you, Beth, to give your Corona bottle head."

Beth smiled at him, glanced at her sister, and then shrugged. She lifted up her glass bottle, closed her eyes, tilted her head to the side, and licked the bottle from the middle up to the top. She licked the side several times and then flicked her tongue lightly on the tip. She parted her lips and took the top of the bottle into her mouth. Peter grew aroused, watching as she wrapped her lips around the bottle and pushed it in and out of her mouth. She opened her eyes and stared at Jerrod as she pulled the bottle out with a pop.

"Me likey!" Jerrod said, applauding spastically.

"My turn!" Beth said, surveying the group. "Scott, truth or dare?"

"Dare," Scott said.

"Dare...dare. I dare you to kiss Maggie."

"Hey!" Peter said.

"Don't worry, Peter. You'll get your turn. Scott, do it."

Peter looked at Maggie. Maggie rolled her eyes then pursed her lips. Scott leaned over and pecked her, holding the kiss for a second.

"Hey!" Peter said, shoving Scott back.

Scott batted him away victoriously.

"Take it easy, tiger. It's just a game," Maggie said. "Okay, my turn. Peter, truth or dare?"

"Truth."

"Truth? Truth…hmm…Okay, big college man. Did you get any Fs this semester?" She looked at him. Fire danced in her eyes.

"No. What? No. Forget it. Dare."

"No, you chose truth," Jerrod said. "My turn."

"No, I changed my mind. I want dare."

"Okay. Dare. Kiss Jerrod," Maggie said.

"Oh, fuck you," Peter said. "Come on, give me something good."

"Fine, homophobe. Go skinny dip in the river."

Peter jumped up and took off his shirt. "Who's with me?"

"It's your dare. Now, does Beth have to help you with those trunks again? Or are you going to take them off?"

"Beth, you want to help me?" Peter asked.

Beth stood up, took off her sweatshirt, and ran toward the water. Peter left his shorts on and chased after her. The rest followed behind. They laughed as they disrobed in the darkness and splashed into the water. Once he was waist deep, Peter threw his swimming trunks back on shore. He swam up to Maggie and bear hugged her, feeling her toned naked body against his. She swatted him away and splashed him in the face.

Beth swam up to Jerrod and hung onto his shoulders as he swam out into deeper water. Jen and Maggie crouched in the water so only their necks and heads were visible. Scott tackled them both, and then they dunked him. Jerrod swam behind the houseboat, with Beth clinging to his back, and then let the current take them around to the edge of the waterslide. He held on to the ladder with one hand and pulled Beth in front of him. They kissed. He held her by the small of her back and pushed his tongue into her open mouth. She straddled his thigh and felt for him beneath the water.

"Guess we know who Beth's hooking up with tonight," Peter said.

"You didn't know they're together?" Jen said, wading over to him.

"I guess I'm out of the loop," Peter said, watching Maggie behind her.

"That's what happens when you move away, Peter," Jen said.

"So what else am I missing? Don't tell me you and Scott are hooking up?"

"You never know," she said playfully.

Their hands touched momentarily as she ran her arms back and forth across the surface of the water. Peter took his eyes way from Maggie and looked at Jen. She had a funny look he couldn't place.

A shriek broke his train of thought. Beth splashed frantically back toward the shore, with Jerrod behind her. She ran up out of the water completely naked, shaking her hands.

"What's wrong?" Maggie asked, wading up to follow her.

"I felt something in the river," she said.

"Ha ha. Yes, sir!" Scott said to Jerrod. "You felt a river snake I bet!"

Beth shook her hands and wildly shook her head. "No, I felt something like a fin on my feet. Oh God, it was gross!"

"It was probably just a fish," Peter said.

"Oh God, just the thought of it—you would be freaked out too. I felt it with both feet. It was big, I think." She stood there, with the fire behind her, staring out into the dark water. "Look! There it is!"

They all hurried out of the water and strained to see.

"I don't see anything, except some shrinkage," Jen said.

The three guys all looked down then covered themselves.

"All right, naked swimming is over. Back to the fire," Maggie said. "Scott, quit staring at us and go get some towels."

Peter peered out for several minutes but couldn't see anything except the black water. A bug bit him on his bare ass. He swatted it then rejoined his friends.

13

An hour later, Peter was clothed, dry, and getting drunk. Scott and Jerrod were reliving the glory days of varsity football. The girls were bringing up their classmates who had already gotten fat in the year since they graduated. Peter thought about Maggie, thought about high school, thought about Colorado.

Jerrod got up with the football, took a running start, and leaped over the fire. The girls applauded gleefully. Scott and Peter both followed, and the boys took turns leaping across the flames. Their shadows twisted wildly up the cliff face. Jerrod tossed the football to Peter, picked up his spear, and danced around the fire pit like a warrior. The fire crackled. Jerrod twirled his weapon above him. The guys danced and chanted, and the girls watched and laughed. The exaggerated shadows stretched up behind them, dancing and writhing like banshees in the summer night. Peter collapsed down next to Maggie and whispered in her ear.

"You want to go out on the boat with me for a few?" he asked.

"No, not with that fish thing swimming around," she said.

"I'm sure that's long gone by now. Don't you want to go?"

"I'm not going back out there tonight," she said.

Peter pulled back and tried to read her face.

"Looks like your beer's almost done. You need another?" she asked.

Peter thought for a moment. "Is something wrong?" he asked quietly.

"No, why? Is something wrong with you?"

"No, it's just…never mind," he said. "Actually, there is something." He waited for a response.

She glanced over at Beth. The rest of the group was listening.

"Why did you ask me about school?"

"What do you mean?"

"When I said 'truth,' you asked me about failing the semester."

"It was just a game. What's the big deal?"

"I dropped out."

"What?" Scott said.

"I dropped out. Did you know?" Peter asked, still looking at Maggie.

"Why are you telling me now?" Maggie asked. "When did this happen?"

"Did you know? Is that why you asked me?"

"No, I didn't know. What have you been doing out there?"

Peter sighed, "I just stopped going. The classes are early. I don't know. It just didn't work out."

"So, are you moving back home?" Jen asked.

"I don't know. I hope not."

"That's nice," Maggie said.

"I didn't mean it like that, Maggie," Peter said. "I don't want to move back in with my parents. That's what I meant."

"No, I know what you meant. You never wanted to live here."

"Look, it's not a big deal. I just haven't told my parents yet, and I was worried everyone might already know somehow."

Maggie stood up and walked away slowly. "Well thanks for not telling me," she said. "I'm going to bed."

"Me too," Beth said.

Jen watched her sister join Maggie as they ducked into their tent. She turned back and caught a glimpse from Scott.

"Well shit," Scott said, smirking, "there's always a nightshift open at the ol' ice cream factory."

"Great," Peter said. "So I can spend the rest of my life watching Marty Luft piss into that jar of maraschino cherries? No thanks."

"It pays the bills," Scott said. "And Marty Luft doesn't work there anymore. He got a job at the prison."

"So, I guess I can't call you Johnny college anymore," Jerrod said. "I'll just start calling you Johnny fuckup."

"Where's that bottle of Jack? I think I'm in need," Peter said, flipping Jerrod the finger.

"I think I'm turning in early myself," Scott said, forcing a yawn. "Jen, can I escort you back to my tent?"

Jen furrowed her brow at Scott and squinted her eyes. Then she raised her eyebrows twice.

"Why, yes," she said, "that would be lovely." She offered up one hand. Scott took it and pulled her up.

"Bomb chick a wow-wow," Jerrod sang.

"You. Shut the fuck up." Jen pointed in his direction as she as Scott walked back toward his tent. Scott unzipped the entrance and offered her to go in first. Jen crawled in, spun around, and plopped down on Scott's sleeping bag. She kicked off her sandals and pulled her legs in. Scott followed, zipped up the tent, and then dove in. Their lips met in the dark, and they kissed passionately. She pulled back and laughed, slightly nervous.

"What?" he whispered.

"Nothing. It's just funny."

"What's funny?" Scott said.

"Nothing, really," she said, pulling him toward her. She cupped his cheek in her hand, and he pulled her close, feeling her spine at the small of her back. He reached up and squeezed her breasts over her dress, and then glided his hand up her thigh. She froze when he reached her panties. He pulled his hand away and touched her face. She kissed his ear, his neck, and ran her hand over his chest.

"I think it's funny that—here I am, the kid sister of Miss Barbie USA making out with the prom king."

"We aren't in high school anymore," Scott said under his breath. "I want to make love to you tonight."

Jen snorted.

"What?" Scott said.

"Easy, tiger," she said. "Let's just do this for a while." She kissed him again.

"Come on, tonight will be perfect. What are you worried about?"

"I'm not worried about anything. I just want to get to know you a little better first, that's all."

Scott plunged back in to kiss her neck.

"Whatever you want," he said, "I'm cool with."

"Thanks," she whispered, and then bit his earlobe. The two lay on top of the sleeping bags, kissing until they fell asleep.

Outside, Peter and Jerrod took turns on the whiskey, trying to listen for any noises coming from Scott's tent.

"You think he's going to seal the deal?" Jerrod said.

"Fuck no. Cock-tease in there? She won't give it up to anyone."

"Just because she wouldn't let you take her shirt off freshman year…This is different. This is pussy magnet number one Scott Hey we're talking about."

"She won't do it. Speaking of not sealing the deal," Peter said, handing his friend the booze, "why aren't you in there with Beth? We both could be getting some right now, but instead we're sitting out here pulling pud."

"Trust me, dude," Jerrod said. "I'm gonna turn that shit out six ways to Sunday."

"Shit."

"Night's still young."

"That it is. That it is. What did Bob Dylan sing? God bless those pretty women?"

"Fuck if I know. Cheers." Jerrod clanked the whiskey bottle against Peter's beer can, and they both took a swig. They watched the fire die down. By the time the fire was out, Peter's mood had lifted. He staggered back to his tent, took a piss, and then unzipped the entrance and crawled in. He took off all his clothes and lay on top of his sleeping bag. As he started to drift, he heard the zipper open.

"Who's there?" he said.

"Shhhh," Maggie said, climbing in. "Be quiet."

He pulled the sleeping bag over his lap.

She pulled it back down and ran a finger up his leg. "Lay back and don't make a sound."

She took off her clothes and crawled on top of him. He pulled her face down to his, and their tongues met. She licked his lips and kissed him deeply. She tasted like smoke. She planted both her hands on his chest and pushed herself up. He palmed her small breasts as she grasped his hard-on. She straddled him, pushing her body down on top of him forcefully. He moaned, and she covered his mouth with her hand. He licked her fingers and held on to her ass as she rode him. She fucked hard, scratching his neck and shoulders. They came together, holding in their cries as best they could. She collapsed on his side, panting.

"Where did that come from?" he said, after a moment.

She put her finger over his lips. "Sweet dreams," she whispered, pulling up her shorts. He watched her get dressed in the darkness, and then she left.

14

Out in the river, under the moonlight, a dark form swam silently toward the campsite. A short stocky man emerged slowly out of the water as his feet touched the sandy river bottom. He walked up the bank until the water was waist deep, and then paused, crouched, and listened. He heard heavy snoring from two of the tents. After he was satisfied that they were asleep, he began moving toward them again, rising up out of the river. A long knife hung from a belt holding up his soaked pants. His shirtless torso was covered with tattoos. Faded images of women and children covered his chest and shoulders, and calligraphy stretched across his abdomen. His left forearm bore a skeleton in a black cowl, wielding a scythe. He pulled the knife out of his belt as he crept up to the smoldering ashes of the fire pit and then paused again. He walked carefully past the tents, up to the cliff face between Scott's tent and Peter's empty hammock. He checked behind him and then squatted. He dug his knife into the earth, where it met the rock, and pushed it in up to the hilt. He repeated the action several yards to his right, and then again a few more feet over, stopping every so often to listen. He knelt down and dug some more, and then used his rough hands to pull away the soil from the rock. He stooped down so his nose was inches away from the hole he made, looked, and sniffed. He swore under his breath. Jesus Reyes stood up straight and craned his neck to look up the rock face towering above. He turned back to the tents, wielding the knife.

15

Peter woke with a killer headache to hear Scott yelling. It was hot in the tent. He pulled on his swimming trunks and stuck his head out for some fresh air. Scott was staring out at the water.

"Dude, trying to sleep. What time is it?"

"The fucking boat's gone."

"What boat?" Peter said slowly.

"Our fucking houseboat is gone," Scott said, and walked over to him.

"What do you mean the houseboat is gone?"

"Well, do you see a houseboat? I don't."

Peter looked. There was, in fact, no houseboat on the water where they had left it. "Shit. No houseboat," Peter said, and fell back into his tent.

"Get up, asshole. We have to go find it."

"Hold on. This is fucked," Peter said. He slowly pulled himself out of the tent and stood up. The three girls were getting out of their tent. He didn't see Jerrod. "Did Jerrod take it?"

"I wish. He's passed out in the hammock. Wake up, Jerrod!" Scott yelled. A groan emerged from behind their tent.

"This is not happening," Maggie said, walking up to the shoreline. "Which one of you tied the boat off yesterday?"

"I did," Peter said. He walked up to the tree he had used. "Look." The rope was still around the tree trunk, the end dangling limp into the water. He pulled twenty feet of wet rope out of the river and held up the frayed end. "This isn't good."

"Jerrod, get the fuck up!" Scott yelled.

"The fucking rope broke?" Beth said. "That's not our fault, is it?"

"I don't know how it could break, it looks pretty new," Peter said, looking carefully at the end.

"Can one of you call the marina?" Scott asked.

"Mine's on the boat," Beth said. "Fuck."

"I've got mine," Maggie said. She dug her phone out of her tent and flipped it open. She looked at the screen and started pacing.

"What?" Beth said.

"No signal."

"You won't get a signal."

"Shut up for a second." She walked up to Peter's tent, then up to the water's edge, and then back to the other grove of trees. "No signal. Jesus Christ."

"Told you."

"Okay, well, shit. How far could it have gone? It would have drifted back downstream, and eventually someone will see it."

"There it is," Peter said.

"Where?" Jen asked.

Peter waded out into the water and pointed downstream. "I can see the rear end of it, must have got stuck in the sand. Thank Christ." They all waded out and could see it had drifted around the bend and was grounded a few hundred yards on their side of the bank. "Scott, let's go get it." The two swam out into the current, leaving their friends knee-deep behind. Peter kicked lazily, and the river propelled him toward the boat. Scott shot past him, and Peter let him go. He kicked a few more times in toward the houseboat and then stood up in the soft mud. He splashed up to the boat, planted both hands on the white side, and pushed. It didn't move. He walked around to the front, lifted himself up, and walked toward the cabin. The glass door was open. He paused.

"What is it?" Scott asked. Peter waved him off, trying to look inside the boat. After a few moments of seeing and hearing nothing, he walked slowly through the doorway. "See anything?" Scott asked, now behind him on the deck.

"No. Shut up," Peter said. He brushed aside the curtain to the bedroom, stuck his head in, and then walked farther down the hall. Nothing was taken that he could see. Nothing looked out of place. "Well, I don't see shit. What do you think?"

"I think we're lucky. Could have been a fuckload worse."

Peter made it to the stern, marched back up to the pilot's chair, and looked at Scott.

"I think you're right. We are lucky." He pointed to the key with the bobber key chain stuck in the ignition. He grabbed the key, turned it over, and the engine started up. He turned the engine back off, and the two jumped back into the mud to push off. This time they both pushed from the font. After a few seconds, the black mud gave way.

Two hours later, the crew was back in open water. The houseboat ran fine, and all their belongings were in order. Peter inspected the extra lines of rope under the seat cushions; they all looked like new. He eventually plopped down on a padded bench in the cabin and ate some powdered donuts. Scott checked the maps periodically and navigated them past some lush green islands. Peter dozed for an hour and then got up to make some lunch. The girls stayed back on the rooftop, sharing sunscreen and soaking in the rays. Jerrod stayed in one of the bed compartments, sleeping off his hangover. By three, the clouds had begun to roll in.

16

That afternoon they pulled up on the muddy shore of one of Bill's approved islands. Jerrod and Peter tied off a line to a tree and checked it repeatedly. After seeing the mud and joking about the disappearing boat, they all decided to skip the tents and sleep on the houseboat. Up a ways, the family from the marina had also docked for the night, and their kids were playing tag. The mosquitoes swarmed the group as they walked into the grass and trees to help with the wood. The girls sprayed each other with repellent and dressed back in their shorts and shirts.

Scott found a patch of grass up from the shore and started gathering dead branches into a pile. While he worked on the fire, Peter took out his fishing rod and tackle box and set up in the back of the boat, facing the water. He pulled a white-and-red bobber out of the top tray of his tackle box, strung it on the line, and then clamped on a lead weight with his needle-nose pliers. He tied a hook to the end after a few threading attempts, and then opened the Styrofoam container to pull out a sluggish earthworm. The worm writhed between his fingers as he baited the hook, and then dangling the worm out over the water to his right. He cast upstream, landing the bobber some twenty feet away. It floated back downstream and then rested where the line pulled it tight. Peter sat back and watched the tree line across the river, feeling the gentle pull of the current on his line. He waited for a few minutes, then reeled it back in, and cast again, this time a little closer in. The bobber floated back down and then dipped out of sight. He felt a nibble and flicked up the rod. The line pulled tight, then slackened. Another nibble and he gave it a good tug. This time he hooked something. He stood up. The rod bent over severely as he pulled up, reeling in. He felt the steady pull, and the line started moving from one side to the other. He stopped for a moment, let out some line, and then started again, pulling up on the rod. He could feel the fish on the hook. He reeled in now, watching where the line plunged through the water. A moment later, he pulled a six-inch catfish out of the river.

"Hey, dinner is served!" Scott said, walking up behind him.

"Look at the size of this monster!" Peter laughed. "The worm was bigger than the fish." He pulled it over the engine cover and held it up close. The fish was a wet black-and-gray color, gills and fins flapping. He grasped it behind the gills, pulled the hook out of its lower lip, and then tossed it back into the water. "You want to try?"

"Nah, I'm going to fish tomorrow," Scott said. "You getting hungry yet?"

"Yeah. I'm going to try once more, then I'll be ready for some more motherfucking hot dawgs."

"Yah, das wieners in das fire, yah, yah," Scott said, walking back through the boat.

Peter pushed the bobber up the line, added another weight, baited the hook again, and cast. He cast three more times, slowly reeling the line back in. On the fourth cast, he had another nibble. He let it alone, and then felt another bite. He jerked up on the rod, and this time he got a big pull. He reeled in, but the line grew taut, and the rod buckled. He let out some line, and all of a sudden the reel was spinning as the line shot out. He fought back, pulling up the fishing pole quickly, and the line snapped in two. He almost fell over backward.

"Goddamn son of a bitch!" He looked out over the dark water in front of the setting sun. "I'll get yous yet, you dirty motherfucker you." He propped his pole up against a corner of the boat and turned to walk in for some dinner. Maggie was moving toward him in the darkness of the boat. The rest of the group was out on the shore, standing around the fire. Peter held up his hands to put around Maggie's waist, but she reached out and slapped him five.

"Let's go up on the roof," she said, passing him in the hall.

He held onto her hand as they walked to the narrow winding stairs. "Ladies first," Peter said, bowing slightly. Maggie went up the stairs, and he grabbed her butt.

"Knock it off, Pete," she said.

"What—not in the mood now?"

She ignored him and finished the stairs with one hand behind, blocking her butt. Peter joined her on the top deck, and the two watched for a moment as the sun set behind the trees.

"This evening air is nice now that it's cooled down a little," he said, for lack of anything better to say. She sighed and nodded.

"Pete, we need to talk," she said. He moved in to kiss her, but she moved away. "Pete, really. Listen to me."

"Okay, jeez," he laughed. "What?"

"I don't know how to say this, so I'm just going to come out with it."

"You pregnant?"

"Will you be serious for one second, please."

"Sorry, I am serious, babe. What do you want to talk about?"

"I've been thinking that we need to enjoy this summer as much as we possibly can."

"I think we're off to a pretty good start so far, don't you?"

"Yeah, absolutely. I mean…I don't know. I think you are interested in other things, and I think you should do what you want this summer."

"I am doing what I want. I'm here with you."

"You know what I mean."

"Actually, no, I don't. What are you saying?"

"Pete, I think we would be better off dating this summer."

"We are dating. We've been dating for three years."

"No, we've been going out for three years. I think we should date."

"What's the difference?" He stepped up to the rail and looked over the waterslide. "You mean you want to date someone else?"

"No, not someone else. God. I just mean date… like…whoever."

"What? Whoever? Where is this coming from?" he heard himself say.

"No, I don't know. I love you, you know. But you're only here for another month, and then I'm still here in Illinois. I'd like to spend time with other people."

"What was last night all about? Jesus, I'm here for six more weeks. I came back to be with you. I can't believe this. Last night you wanted to fuck. Now you want to break up?"

"Peter, I wanted your penis last night. You didn't like it? We're not breaking up. I just want to talk to you about dating. What's wrong with dating? Don't you want to have fun with other people? Don't you want to date any girls in Denver?"

"Who have you been dating besides me?"

"No one. That's not the point. The point is I want to have fun this weekend, and I still have feelings for you, but I think you should go back to Colorado without strings attached. What's so bad about that?"

"Well, I might not be going back now. So, we're fine. I'll be here, and you'll be here, and we'll be fine."

"That still doesn't change anything, Peter. Just think about it. I'm going back down now. You want to come with me?"

"Jesus fucking Christ. Whatever." He turned his back to her and stared out at the water. She climbed down the ladder. He waited ten minutes, walked through the boat, and joined Scott and Jerrod out by the fire.

"What's your problem?" Scott asked.

"I don't have a fucking problem. Give me a beer," Peter said.

Scott fetched him a can. "Well, you look all pissy," Scott said.

"Well, I look all pissy because Maggie just broke up with me, apparently, and I'm a little pissed off right now."

"Oh, sorry dude," Scott said. "Does that mean she's available?"

Peter coldcocked him in the chin as hard as he could. Jerrod jumped up off his haunches. Scott didn't fall over, but lurched to his side. He slowly turned, glaring at Peter and rubbing his chin.

"What the fuck was that?" he said, taking deliberate steps in Peter's direction.

"She's not fucking available. She's my girlfriend!" He swung. Scott stepped out of his way and then returned with a punch in the side. Peter felt a sting. Scott kneed him in the groin and then punched him in the face. Peter fell back into the mud.

"Stop it!" Jen shouted from the bow of the boat, looking down at the fight. "Jerrod, do something!"

Jerrod laughed.

"This is between those two, not me," he said, looking over Scott's back to see Peter lying on the ground.

Scott hunched over Peter. "Are you done, motherfucker?"

"Get off me!" Peter rolled over on his stomach and then lunged up into Scott's midsection. Peter pushed Scott back with his legs until Scott tripped over a branch, and the two fell back to the ground. Scott got Peter in a headlock and pinned him to the dirt.

"Are you done now?" he panted.

"Get off of me, dammit," Peter yelled.

Scott waited for a few breaths, then loosened his grip and stood up. Peter stumbled over to the fire, took another beer out of the cooler, and plopped down. He chugged half the beer and then scowled. Jerrod said nothing. Scott pulled himself up into the boat, and Maggie and Jen followed him into the cabin. Jerrod grabbed a beer and sat down next to Peter.

"What the fuck are you looking at?" Peter sneered, aching.

"A stupid son of a bitch," Jerrod said.

"Oh yeah, how's that?"

"You're lucky Scott didn't crush you, mofo. It's not his fault you just got dumped."

"Fuck you." He finished his beer and then reached for another. "I could've taken him."

"Yeah, right. He was kicking your ass, bro. Serious. You're okay though, right?"

"I'm great, what do you think?" Peter said, and took a swig. As he looked up, he saw a dark form standing on the other side of the fire.

Jerrod saw it too and jumped up. "Who's there?" Jerrod stepped back, and Peter stood up painfully.

"Hey guys, it's your neighbor up the beach. Take it easy," the form said. He walked closer, and the fire lit his face. "Could you guys try to keep it down? We've got kids trying to go to sleep. We can hear you partying from inside our boat."

"Oh," Peter said, and collapsed back on the ground.

"Who's the adult here?" the man asked, looking down at Peter and then at Jerrod.

"We are," Jerrod said.

"You boys old enough to be drinking?"

"Yes, you want one?" Peter opened the cooler lid.

"No, I better be getting back. The wife's got some fish cooking."

"You catch any?"

"Yeah, couple catfish. Actually, I will have a beer if you don't mind." He walked around and fished a can out of the cooler. "You guys catch anything today?"

"No," Peter said. The man squinted at Peter.

"You okay? Your face looks a little messed up." He took a swig and kept his eyes on Peter.

Jerrod kept standing.

"I'm fine, we were just messing around."

"I'm a doctor, if you need me to take a look at anything."

"He said he was fine," Jerrod said.

The doctor looked at him, and then took another swig. "Thanks for the beer. I'm heading back. I'd appreciate it if you guys kept it down tonight."

"No problem, asshole," Jerrod muttered under his breath.

Peter stared into the white embers in the flames. The man looked up at the smoke, then turned and walked into the darkness.

As Dr. Bain walked back up the shoreline, he watched for branches and listened to the bugs humming in the night air. Halfway back to his family, he heard a rustling in the bushes. He stopped and looked, but couldn't make out anything. Up above, the moon barely shone through the clouds. He took another step, and the bushes moved again, this time closer. He quickened his pace, and tree limbs started to shake up and down the beach. He saw the light from his boat and broke out into run. The bushes exploded with motion, leaves shaking and branches whipping as he ran clumsily over the rocks and dried mud. The bugs had stopped buzzing, and he heard a new noise behind him, like wheezing. He looked over his shoulder. His foot caught on a gnarled root. He plummeted face-first onto a rock. He tried to stand up, but dazed, fell back down. Something trickled into his eyes. He wiped his face and felt a sticky, hot liquid. He tried to see his boat but couldn't see the light anymore. He stumbled against a tree trunk. The branches were shaking furiously. Wheezing, more wheezing, and then a horrible croaking came from behind him. He spun around and a massive shape loomed in front of him. The stench hit him first, and then a jagged machete swung out of the night and smashed into his head, splitting his skull on impact. The last thing he saw was the black form swooping on him as he fell to the ground.

17

The night air was still. The bushes and trees posed silently on the island shore, and the bugs resumed humming. The form straddled the fresh corpse, hacking away at the face and neck with the rusted blade until the head tore off and rolled away. The thing tossed the machete aside, grasped the head, and hungrily devoured the gaping neck meat. It tore the cheeks and lips off the skull with its teeth, chomping and grunting as it swallowed. Eventually it stood up, retrieved the weapon, and dragged the carcass into the bushes. At the base of a large chestnut tree, the form dropped the wet ragged mess and hacked a cavity in the chest. It immediately set about feasting on the shredded intestines. It wheezed and gobbled and belched in the darkness. It pried open the rib cage with its gore-drenched fingers, and then buried its teeth deep into the bloody cavity, gulping viciously. Three more stinking forms descended on the kill, one tearing through the thigh meat then successfully jerking a leg clean off the body. Within half an hour, the three disappeared, leaving only a bloody pile of shit and bones behind.

18

"Hey, Peter, want to come play some cards?" Jen asked from the deck.

Peter sat cross-legged by himself next to the crackling fire. He stared into the flames and ignored her.

"Peter, are you just going to sit there all night?" She leaned over the rail and looked into the dark trees behind him.

"I'm fine, thanks," he said.

"We're gonna play Asshole."

"I'm okay. Maybe in a little while."

"We need six people."

"You can play with five."

"Yeah but five sucks. Come on."

"Maggie just dumped me. So I don't feel like playing Asshole, okay?"

"Okay, sorry I asked," she sighed, and walked back to the cabin. As she slid the glass door open, "Killing Me Softly" played into the night air from the small TV speakers.

Peter shook his head and stood up. "What the fuck?" he asked himself out loud, looking through the glass at the group sitting around the table. "What's wrong with me?" He walked slowly down the beach, away from their neighbors. He thought about the last few times he spent with Maggie and searched for clues that would have predicted this. He kicked a rock on the dirt and stubbed his toe. He swore under his breath, slapped a mosquito on the back of his neck, and looked up for stars. There weren't any. He wondered when all the clouds had rolled in. It had been clear when it was still light out. He thought it smelled like rain. The scent of rain mixed with the dead fish smell of the river. A low horn moaned in the distance from a barge, slipping through the night. He heard something close to him in the brush and stopped. A chill went through him, and his heartbeat quickened. After a moment of silence, he took a deep breath and kept walking.

Behind the row of trees, out of sight, a pair of red eyes blinked. The eyes were low to the ground, amid the underbrush. As Peter moved along the shore, the eyes followed, surrounded by a dark mass. The eyes followed almost silently, weaving expertly between the twigs and branches. Peter paused again, this time turning toward the trees and straining his eyes to make out anything. The eyes and the form quietly withdrew into darkness. There was a splash in the river. Peter spun around but couldn't see anything. Up ahead the tree limbs blocked his path up the shore, so he turned and headed back to the boat. The eyes followed.

When he walked in, the five were all slamming beers at once. Jerrod put his beer down, then Jen, then Scott, then Maggie, and finally Beth, gasping.

"You asshole!" she said after taking a breath.

"That's my job. I'm the asshole!" Jerrod proclaimed triumphantly. "Beware the wrath of the waterfall!"

"Payback's a bitch," Scott said. "Hey, Peter, you want in?"

"All right, I'm ready to play," he said, sitting down on the captain's stool.

Scott leaned over the table and extended a hand. "We good?"

"No, but I'm ready to play," Peter said, slapping his hand out of the way.

"Good enough. We're already in place, so you're vice-ass," Scott said.

"Vice-ass, deal me in."

"Wait," Beth said. "You're vice-ass."

"So?"

"So that makes you beer bitch."

"Oh, right. Who needs one?"

"Beer me, beer bitch!" Jerrod shouted.

Peter stood back up and walked out to fetch the beers. They all chanted "beer bitch" and pounded their fists on the table until he came back. He handed them out and then cracked one open for himself.

"Drink two for coming late to the game," Jerrod said.

"Fuck you, asshole. You drink two," Peter replied.

"Easy, killer. Asshole has supreme power until the cards are dealt, remember? So make it three."

Peter drank three and shut up. The cards were dealt. President and asshole exchanged their best and worst two cards. Then vice president and Peter exchanged their single best and worst. After several cards were played, they started arguing over whether a single two could beat doubles, and if you could play triples over singles.

Jen's mix CD ended, and she put in the *80s Monsters of Rock* disc. "The Final Countdown" farted through the TV speakers at full volume, and Maggie became president. She made everyone drink, except Peter, and wouldn't look at him. Peter looked up to see Beth staring at him. She turned away when their eyes met. After the second round, they broke out the no-longer-ice-cold bottle of Jägermiester, and each took a swig as they passed it around.

"So what kind of fish did you catch, Peter?" Beth asked.

"I didn't catch anything," he replied, slurring slightly.

"I thought I saw you catch something."

"A tiny catfish. I threw it back."

"Are you going to cook the catfish if you catch a big one?"

"Yeah, when I catch some, we'll all eat catfish."

"I won't. I'm a vegetarian," Beth announced.

"Don't you eat fish?" Jerrod asked.

"No, I don't eat fish. I'm a vegetarian. I don't eat meat."

"Vegetarians eat fish. My cousin eats fish, and she's a vegetarian," Jerrod said.

"Your cousin Melissa? She's a cunt. And she's not a vegetarian," Jen said.

"Whoa, easy. Little hostility there, Jen?" Jerrod said.

"No. Just facts. One, Melissa Blanchette is a stupid bitch. And B, you can't be a vegetarian if you eat fish."

"Well, why the hell don't you eat fish?"

"I do. I'm not a vegetarian. Beth is."

"Sorry. Beth, why don't you eat fish?"

"Because fish are gross. Why do you care so much what I eat?"

"I don't. You brought it up. Jen, you a vegetarian too?"

"Hell no. I love meat."

"But you're a hippie. Aren't you all vegan or some shit?"

"Yeah, I'm a dirty hippie. I only eat twigs, and I don't shave my legs."

"Wow, Beth," Jerrod said. "Your sister's a little edgy tonight. Maybe she needs to bust out the KB and mellow out man."

"Just because she's got those nasty-ass dreads, doesn't mean she's a hippie," Beth said.

"Oh fuck you, bitch. You said you thought I looked pretty," Jen said, mockingly offended.

"All right, change of subject," Beth said. "She's embarrassed. Did you guys hear about that fish in the Amazon that swims up your pee hole?"

The guys shouted at the same time and covered their privates.

"What the hell! Pee hole?" Peter exclaimed. "That's an urban legend."

"No, it's true," Beth said. "We watched this show on the nature channel with our dad. These little tiny fish swim up your urine stream and then lodge themselves in your urethra." The two sisters both beamed with excitement. "They have these barbs they stick out once they're up in there, so they can't come out, and then they start gnawing their way up your urethra. One guy had surgery, and they found one five inches long, all engorged on the guy's wiener."

"Well, I'm never swimming again," Scott said, throwing down his hand.

"Hey, keep playing!" Jerrod said.

"Nah, this is getting old. Fucking wiener fish—what a bunch of bullshit."

"It's true," Beth said. She unscrewed the cap on the Jägermiester and lifted up the bottle. "To the wiener fish!" she toasted, and then took a swig.

Peter reached for the bottle, but Beth dropped it out of her hand onto the table. It landed with a thud, and thick black liquid splashed out over the cards. Peter started to swear, and then saw her face, staring past him. He turned around. Someone stood wild-eyed right on the other side of the glass door, reaching for the handle.

They all jumped up. Peter darted over to the kitchen drawer to grab a knife. The door flew open, and the intruder stepped into the light of the cabin. It was the woman from the other boat on the island. She looked crazed, confused, and squinted to adjust her eyes to the light.

"Lady, you're in the wrong boat," Scott said, standing in front of Maggie.

The lady stood in the doorway, staring at them. She was crying. Behind her, out on the deck, her two children peered in nervously.

"Guys, easy," Jen said. "Are you okay?"

"My husband is gone. Have you seen him?"

"He's gone? No, no, we haven't seen anyone," Jen said.

"We did, yeah. We did see him, a couple hours ago," Peter said. "He stopped by our campfire for a while, and then he walked back to you."

"Oh God. He never came back. He never came back." She was frantic. Peter put down the knife and ran his fingers through his hair. The woman stared at him. "You did something to him," she said.

"What?"

"You did something to him." She lifted a finger and pointed in Peter's face. "I know."

"Whoa, settle down. I just told you what happened."

"What did you do?" she screamed, shaking and crying. Jen stepped in between them. "Maybe you should come outside, we can talk this through," she said, trying to put her arm around the woman. The woman jumped back, flailing her arms wildly.

"Stay away from me! You all stay away from my family! I'm calling the cops!" The children started crying, still standing out on the boat deck. She told them to keep quiet. She pulled her cell phone out of her back pocket and dialed 911.

"We didn't do anything to your husband," Maggie said. "We want to help you, if you'll calm down."

The lady glared at Maggie, holding the phone up to her ear.

"Can you get a signal?" Jen asked.

The women stared in silence. The whole boat listened. After a minute she slowly put the phone away and backed toward the door.

"You're going to pay. You all know something. You can tell your lies to the police!" With that, she spun around and walked briskly out to the deck, gathering her children.

"You're crazy!" Jerrod yelled.

Jen pushed him and told him to shut up.

"Just wait until the authorities get here!" she shouted, as she jumped down onto the beach, and then pulled each kid off, one by one. The three disappeared into the dark.

"Jesus fucking Christ," Peter said, looking at the rest of the group.

"What are we going to do?" Maggie asked. Beth sat at the table crying.

"What? What are you crying about?" Peter asked.

"Leave her alone," Maggie said. "What are we going to do?"

"What the fuck do you keep asking me for?" Peter said, picking up the liquor bottle. "She's in hysterics. Her husband is fine. We just saw him."

"Did you guys do anything to him?" Jen asked.

"No! What the fuck?" Jerrod said. "You heard Peter. We gave him a fucking beer, and he walked back to his boat."

"Well, he obviously didn't make it. Did you see him walk all the way back?"

"No. Jesus," Peter said. "We saw him walk away toward his boat. Once he walked away from the fire, we couldn't see him anymore."

"Well, should we go look for him?"

"No," Peter said. "The last fucking thing we should do is get involved. Everyone should just chill."

"I'm going to go look for him," Beth said, standing up. "Can someone come with me?"

"I'll go with you," Maggie said.

"So will I." Scott pulled a flashlight out of his backpack.

"This is ridiculous," Peter said. "Whatever. Go have fun."

"You're a real hero, Peter," Maggie said.

"Fuck you." Peter stepped back and walked to the other end of the boat.

The group gathered their flashlights, put on their rain jackets and then set off into the night, the light beams rolling across the tree trunks and rocks. Jerrod lingered for a moment at the front of the boat and then jumped down and followed the rest of the group.

Peter watched the lights move up the beach, feeling a chill as the rain splashed on his neck and shoulders. He took a drink and stared into the darkness. "God fucking dammit," he said, and then walked back to grab his gear. He jumped off the front and ran to catch up with his friends, watching to avoid branches and rocks. As he caught up with them, he counted four lights. One of the flashlights pointed into his eyes.

"Maggie?" Scott asked into the darkness.

"No. Peter," he panted.

"Where's Maggie?"

"You tell me. She was with you."

"You didn't pass her just now?"

"No."

The whole group circled around him. Scott walked up face to face and looked into his eyes.

"You're telling me you didn't just see her? She went back to the boat to get her jacket. You couldn't have missed her."

"It's fucking dark, man. Maybe she didn't want to talk to me." Scott looked at him, and then turned to Beth and Jen. "Okay, we need to find Maggie. Everyone back to the boat."

"But what about the guy?" Jen asked.

"This is getting stupid. We need to stay together. Let's go find Maggie, and then we'll worry about the guy."

"Maybe she's with the guy," Jerrod said.

"Shut up!" Beth said. "This isn't funny. Yeah, back to the boat."

Peter shook his head, turned, and started walking back up the shore.

"Maggie? Where are you?" Jen called. Beth joined in.

They walked around the bend and made it back to the boat within minutes. The girls went through the rooms of the boat, and Jerrod went up to the rooftop. Scott jogged up the shore, shouting periodically for her, but no one heard a noise. A half an hour later, he came back to find them sitting around the table.

"Well, what are you sitting there for? We need to find her!"

"We need to call the cops." Jen rubbed tears out of her eyes. "Where could she have gone?"

"We can't call the cops," Peter said. "We're on this boat with Maggie's fake ID. Besides, no one can get a fucking signal out here."

"So what, Peter? What if she's in trouble?" Beth asked. "What if she's hurt?"

"She's fine, she probably just wants to be alone," Scott said. "I'm sure she's fine."

"Look at how hard it's raining," Jen said. Peter looked at the rain bombarding the deck. A bolt of lightning cracked through the sky, and thunder boomed seconds after. "I don't have a signal," Jen said, looking at her flip phone. "No bars."

"All right, so forget the cops. Let's call the marina," Beth said.

"Yeah, call the marina on the radio," Jen said. "They can bring out a search boat or something."

"What do we tell them?" Peter asked.

"We tell them our friend is missing, and that some guy on the other boat is missing. God, are you stupid?"

"Fine, okay. I'll call the marina." Peter said. "She's going to show up the minute they come out here."

"Good, so call!"

"I'll do it," Scott said. He walked over to the steering column and picked up the speaker of the CB radio. He held down the button and said, "Mayday! Mayday! Come in! Anyone there?" Silence on the other end. "Hello, hello, this is houseboat thirteen, from Mac's Marina. We need some help, can you hear me?" Again, silence. He tried a third time, and then something came back.

"Mac's Marina...switch over to channel five. Repeat. Channel five."

Scott turned the dial and waited.

"This is the marina, what's the trouble?"

"Yes, hello. We are pulled up on the island we were told to stay the night on. Someone from our group is missing. We've looked all over the island and don't know where she is. Can you send someone to help us?"

"Who am I speaking with?" the man on the other end asked.

"This is Scott. Hey." Scott released the button and turned to his friends. "What name did we check the boat out under?"

"Fuck. Umm, she used her fake." Peter said.

"What was the name on the fake?"

"Greene, I think. Stacey…or Sharon maybe?"

"I'm with the party that checked out the boat under Greene. Can you please come help. We've lost one of our party!" Scott held his breath.

"Just hang tight. We'll get someone up there as soon as we can. Maybe half an hour tops. Turn your lights on and stay in your boat."

"Okay, will do," Scott said, and put the receiver back down. Peter and Jerrod nodded and then turned to the window. Jen and Beth were crying, with their heads in their hands.

Nearly an hour went by. Jerrod started to play a Steve Miller CD, but Beth told him to turn it off after a few bars of "Going to the Country." The rain kept pouring. Scott paced up and down the cabin, trying to get a signal on his phone. He tried the CB again but didn't hear anything but static. Peter sat in a corner, drinking beer and watching the rain splash on the window.

"I'm going out again," Scott said, breaking the silence. Beth looked up at his face. "I'm sure she found shelter under some tree or something and is just waiting for the rain to let up."

"The guy told us to stay on the boat," Jen said.

"That was an hour ago. They might be having problems getting here. Who knows if they're even coming."

"We should stay together," Beth said.

"Yeah, but someone needs to stay with the boat when they do show up," Peter said.

"I'll stay here," said Jerrod. "I think we are wasting a great party night. You guys go ahead and do another search, and I'll hold down the fort. Ladies, do you want to stay with me or go out in the rain again?"

Beth and Jen conferred with each other, and then turned back to the boys. "We'll stay here with Jerrod. Be safe."

"Pete, you coming with me?"

"Yeah, what the hell, I'm going crazy waiting for those assholes." Peter pulled a large bowie knife out of his pack and attached the sheath to his belt. "My dad got this for me when I was ten."

"You going to kill us a deer while you're out there?" Jerrod asked.

"You never know," Peter said. He and Scott donned their rain jackets, turned on the flashlights, and wandered back into the night.

19

Ten minutes after their lights faded into the island, Beth saw some red and white lights coming toward them on the water. "Someone's here!"

Jerrod and Jen ran out to the back where Beth was standing. The three watched the lights approaching.

"I don't think they're from the marina," Jerrod said. "They're coming from the wrong direction."

"Maybe they overshot us and had to circle back around," Jen said.

"Maybe. But maybe not. Hello?" Jerrod called out. The lights kept getting closer. Now they could see red and green lights, but still no boat.

"Hello, are you from the marina?" Beth called out. A boat horn blasted, and then a hull appeared just feet away from them.

"Oh, shit, they're going to hit us—get back!" Jerrod pushed the girls back into the cabin, and they ran up toward the kitchen.

With a massive lurch, the three went sprawling into the walls as the bow of the oncoming boat crashed into them. The boxes and bags on the counter spilled out onto the floor, the TV toppled over inches from Jerrod's head. He looked at the TV, dazed, and then pulled himself up.

"Are you okay?" He walked over to Beth. She nodded.

Jen stood up and held her wrist. "Holy shit," she said, panting. "I think I may have broken something."

The three looked at each other then turned simultaneously toward the back. They couldn't hear anything except the rain. Jerrod put his finger to his lips and motioned for them to stay up front. He crept back up the corridor and peered out. Jen and Beth watched his eyes and face slowly look upward.

"Holy shit!" he exclaimed, standing up straight. "You killed our boat!"

"Sorry!" Mandy waved from the bow of her boat, now wedged up into the boat on the shore.

Jerrod walked out as far as he could and inspected the gnarled hulls of both ships.

"Sorry? Are you crazy? You could have killed us!" Beth yelled. "Holy shit, look at our boat!"

"Holy fucking shit is right," Jerrod repeated. "Jesus Christ, look at that hole," he said, pointing to a gaping crack where the boats had made impact. A man stuck his head over the ledge.

"Oh shit." He jumped out into the shallow water and started to push his boat back into the water. He was stumbling.

"I don't know if your boat will float anymore, man," Jerrod said.

"Honey, be careful," Mandy said. Her friend, Karen, walked out, and the other guy.

"Are you all okay?" Beth asked.

"Yeah, we're all right," Karen said. "Are you kids okay? I told them to try beaching farther up, but Mister Man here wouldn't listen, would he?" She crossed her arms and looked at him.

"The river is not navigable," the man said. "I'm real sorry, kids. I hope none of you are hurt. My insurance will cover this, don't worry." He jumped down and walked over to Jerrod, now standing on the shore. "I'm Gary Frette. What's your name?" He stuck out his hand.

"Richard," Jerrod said, shaking it.

"Sorry about your boat, Richard."

"Yeah, I think my girlfriend's wrist is broken. Is your insurance going to pay for that?"

"Oh, Jesus, I'm sorry. I lost control in that current. I thought we had plenty of room."

"You're drunk," Mandy said with a haughty laugh.

"Shut up, woman!" Joe said, still trying to push. "Can you guys help me push this out?" The three men pushed with their shoulders, digging the mud with their heels. "You two, get down off the boat," Joe barked, and held up a hand. Mandy and Karen took turns hopping down, and then the men pushed again. While they struggled, the two women joined Beth and Jen back up in the kitchen, now firmly planted three more feet up into the shore.

"So, you guys been drinking?" Jerrod asked as they grunted.

"What do you think, son. Of course we've been drinking," Gary said.

"Shut up, Gary. No, we haven't. Why don't you mind you're fucking business, kid," Joe snarled.

"Easy, man. I'm just trying to make conversation. We lost one of our friends tonight, you know."

"Shit, sorry about this. You think she drowned?"

"Fuck, man, I hope not. Our other friends are out looking for her."

The three stepped back and inspected their progress. None. The boats were stuck together like two wolves post-coitus. "The other boat up the island is missing someone too. It's kind of fucked up. And now this," Jerrod said.

"I said I was fucking sorry," Joe said. "You think we don't feel bad about it?"

"I'm just saying."

"And I'm just saying…" Joe paused. "Watch it."

"Marina guys were supposed to be here hours ago," Jerrod said, changing the subject. "You see any other boats out on the water?"

"No, we couldn't see shit."

"Well, you want to get out of this rain? We've got some booze if you want to wait it out?"

"Hell yes," Gary said. "I think we could all use a little something for the nerves. What do you say, Joe?"

"I'm staying with my boat. You go ahead," Joe said, and pulled himself back up over the side.

Jerrod and Gary climbed up the front and then opened the sliding door to find the girls laughing at the table.

"What's so funny?" Jerrod asked. Mandy hiccupped, and the four women giggled. Jen was still holding her wrist but seemed to be over it.

"Beth here was telling us about the horrible break-up with your friends Maggie and Peter. Does your friend Peter have anger issues?"

"Whatever," Jerrod said, picking up a beer from the floor. He opened the can, and beer sprayed out into the kitchen.

Mandy shrieked, "Oh my!"

Jerrod slid the glass door open and chucked the can out into the night.

"It's just horrible that we ran into you. Seriously. I want you kids to know that we will pay for whatever damages we may have caused."

"And whatever beer we drink," Karen chimed in.

"You're awfully friendly all of a sudden," Jerrod said.

Gary looked at his wife, and then at Jerrod.

"You two know each other?" he asked.

Jerrod opened another beer, slowly, so it didn't explode, and then handed it to Gary.

"Yep, we go way back. She your wife?" He opened another one and took a drink.

"Yes, she is."

"Easy, big man," Karen said. "We met Richard and his friends earlier today, at the winery. They were very gentlemen-like."

Gary took another drink, assessing the situation. "Well, fuck me running. You got anything harder than Miller Light?"

"Jäger," Beth said. She pulled the bottle from under the table, took a swig, and then handed it to Gary.

He reached across the table. Then an engine howled out on the river.

"Hey, Joe!" he yelled. "Oh shit, Joe!" He ran toward the back, but halfway out, the engine screamed, and the whole boat lurched sideways.

Gary slammed against the bathroom door, crashing into the sink. The boat jolted again, tossing everyone out of their seats. Gary pulled himself up and stumbled out to see the boat on the river push up farther onto the wreckage. "Joe, stop!" he shouted.

But Joe couldn't hear him. Joe slammed it into reverse and pushed the throttle down as far as it could go. He cranked the wheel, and his vessel finally broke free. He put it in neutral and ran out onto the deck.

"Get in! What the hell are you guys doing! Come on!"

"Joe, what the fuck! You're going to sink! Jump off!" Gary yelled.

"It's fine, come on! Get the women! Let's get the fuck out of here!"

Mandy, Karen, Jerrod, Gary, Beth, and Jen all stood huddled together on the stern of houseboat number thirteen, watching Joe drift away into the night.

"Pull back up on shore!" Mandy yelled. "It's not safe to take out! We should stay here until the marina comes to help!"

"Look! The boat's fine. Wade out into the water, I'll come around and pick you up. Come on!" Joe yelled. He went back into the cabin, put the boat in gear, and turned the wheel so he could loop back around. "Fucking idiot wife," he muttered. "Hey, I've got an idea," he said in a high-pitched whine. "Let's go have drinks with the teenagers we just almost killed. I'm a fucking retard bitch. Let's wait for the police to come arrest us!"

Mandy, Gary, and Karen climbed out and slowly waded into the black water, shivering from the rain. They watched their houseboat fade into the river, the white light just visible from the back of the boat. Jerrod squinted to watch from up on their boat, standing next to Jen and Beth. Then the white light disappeared.

"Where did it go?" Jen asked.

"He's coming back around," Beth said.

"No, he isn't," Jerrod answered. They watched the rain in the wind for over five minutes.

"You piece of shit!" Mandy eventually yelled toward the river. "Thanks a lot, you prick!"

The three waded back to shore, and Gary helped the women up into the beached houseboat.

20

Joe continued to swear to himself as he spun the boat around on the water. He heard something behind him, so he killed the engine to listen. Just the rain.

"Goddamn smart ass kid. 'You guys been drinking?' What the fuck. I'll show you some manners, you goddamn punk."

He heard a noise again from the back. He shut up. He noticed a smell, like dead fish. Then he heard something like breathing, deep and raspy. "Who's there?"

More breathing. The hairs on his arms stood up, and his heart started beating through his chest. He looked outside and couldn't see a thing except black water. He noticed the water looked like it was splashing up on the deck. He noticed the surface was way too high, but then he noticed the sound behind him was louder. He jumped around. "Who the fuck is on this boat?"

Two red eyes peered at him from the back of the boat, and the horrid stench of dead flesh engulfed him.

"Get the fuck out of here!" he yelled, running toward the intruder.

The black form was short, like a child. It sprung up and leapt through the cabin, hitting Joe midair. Joe collapsed to the floor, shitting his pants on impact. "Get off me, get off!" He screamed in terror.

The kid attacked like a wild animal, clawing his eyes, biting his nose and ears. Joe grasped for his pocketknife and fumbled to open the blade. A small hand with razor-sharp fingernails snatched the knife away, and then the blade plunged into his chest. The little monster was shredding and biting with unholy strength and tearing through his shirt and skin and ribcage now. Joe shrieked and gurgled as sharp little teeth devoured and gulped his flesh and pulled his viscera out into the open, yanked it away, and spit intestines onto his face. He covered his head, but his forearms were broken and split away, his face torn off, his skull exploded, and his brains splattered with blood and bone about the cabin floor.

Black water surged into the cabin as the boat began to sink. The blood-covered demon-child feasted on the remains for another minute, then scampered back out to the stern, which was now the highest point out of water. It vomited an unbelievable spew of gore into the current and then dove into the deep. The boat disappeared into the Illinois River. Soon after, a dark head broke the surface of the water, and it started swimming toward the island shore, not making a ripple or sound.

21

Scott and Peter found a break in the trees up the shoreline and started trouncing through the scrub. They bent and broke branches as they entered. Wet thorns and brambles ripped at their legs. After a while, a gravel trail opened up at their feet, and they were able to walk unobstructed through the middle of the island. Peter's shins stung, and briars stuck into his skin. He paused to pull them out and then started walking down the narrow trail. Tall trees loomed high above them, giving them a canopy of leaves, sheltering them from the rain. The two walked slowly, shining their flashlights back and forth into the bushes to see any sign of trails branching off.

"Sorry about earlier," Peter said.

"Yeah, I was just joking, you know."

"I don't know what came over me. I was mad at Maggie, and embarrassed. I was just filled with a crazy rage all of a sudden—"

"Wait," Scott interrupted him. They both stopped in their tracks. Peter cocked his head and listened. They looked at each other.

"Do you hear…," Scott whispered, "music?"

A sound could barely be heard up the trail. They both held their breath.

"Yeah, it sounds like a guitar or something."

"Okay, I think it's coming from up there. Turn your flashlight off."

They both clicked off into total darkness and crept softly up the trail. As they approached, the music became discernible. Soon they could clearly hear someone strumming an acoustic guitar. Then they heard some drums, slowly pattering to the tune of the chords.

"I think I recognize that song," Peter whispered.

"Look," Scott pointed, standing a few steps in front.

Peter walked up, and they both could see a light coming from a cabin in the middle of the woods. The light cast a silhouette around three dark forms sitting on the porch. As their eyes adjusted to the light, they could see two of the people playing instruments. One had a small guitar, and the other was squatting over a kettledrum. The third looked like a woman, her head swaying back and forth to the slow jam.

"Hello?" Peter called as he walked up to the cabin. The music stopped abruptly. Peter stopped walking.

"Hey, guys," the woman greeted them cheerfully. It was Maggie. "Aren't they good?"

"Maggie, holy shit," Scott said, rushing up to her. "Are you okay?"

Peter followed closely behind, keeping his eyes on the two musicians. As he walked up to the porch, he saw them clearly. One was sitting on an old wooden chair, holding a tiny guitar. He had long dreadlocks. They looked red or brown, he couldn't tell. The man looked a few years older than him. He had a long goatee and wore a dirty pair of jean overalls. His bare white arms were covered with nasty-looking sores and big freckles. The guy with the drum looked a little younger, with shorter dreadlocks and bushy muttonchops. He also had red-and-brown scabs covering his hands and arms. Peter nodded to him, and he snickered.

"I'm great. I'd like you to meet my new friends." She stood up. "This is Ben and Abe," she said, pointing to each in turn. "They're brothers, and they live on this island. Isn't that cool?"

"Hi, I'm Scott." He reached out a hand.

Ben and Abe both laughed. "Hey, man, what are you guys doing out in the rain?"

"We were looking for her," Peter said.

"She's right here, man," Abe said with a strange half smirk. "She's with us. You guys like to party?"

"Maggie, we should get back to the boat. The others are worried that something happened to you."

"What? But I'm having a great time here. You guys should go bring them back. These two are amazing musicians. Play that last song again, I loved it."

"Are you down?" Ben said, without looking at anyone in particular. Abe giggled and beat the drum a few times.

"Down for what?"

"Are you down with the hootie-hooch?" Ben laughed, and pulled out a joint from behind his ear. Peter looked at Scott then shrugged.

"Well shit, so you guys are like island hippies or something," he said.

They both exploded into laughter, and Maggie joined in.

"Don't be rude, Peter." Maggie took the joint from Ben and lit up. She took a toke and passed it to Scott. "This is really good shit, even better than the shit I have. Let's just chill out here for a while and listen to some sweet tunes."

Scott took a hit and passed it to Peter. He paused and then took a drag.

"What is this shit?" he asked, hacking up the smoke.

The brothers and Maggie all laughed in unison.

"Hah-haught, don't Bogart it, man," Abe said. "That's some homegrown shit right there."

Peter coughed again and handed the joint down to Abe. He took a hit, handed it to his brother, and then started playing his drum again.

"You guys like the Dead?" Ben asked.

"The Dead?" Scott asked.

"The Grateful Dead, man. You like the Grateful Dead?"

"Oh, sure," Scott said, sitting down.

Peter sat down next to him, and the two brothers started playing. Ben strummed what turned out to be a ukulele, and his brother softly kept rhythm on the drum. Peter watched the rain drip off the patio roof, listened to the tune, and waited to feel the effects of the pot. He waved it off the second time around, so Scott and Maggie took turns until it was cashed. Maggie closed her eyes and smiled, swaying her head to the music.

"I guess I get to party with hippies all weekend after all," Maggie said to no one.

"Oh yeah?" Peter asked. She didn't answer back but kept smiling. Scott stared out into the night, the rain looked like it was letting up.

Peter still didn't feel anything, except a burning in his throat. He turned and watched the two brothers, seemingly immersed in their playing. His thoughts drifted back to Maggie and Scott, so he tried to take his mind off the situation by looking around the patio, and then through the crack in the door into the cabin. He could see an old table leg on what seemed to be a dirt floor. Garbage or clothes were piled up on the floor behind the table. It looked like branches mixed with canvas bags, or something. He couldn't quite see. The chair leg moved all of a sudden, and he realized he was looking at someone's leg.

"Who all lives out here with you guys?" he asked, turning back to Ben.

Ben looked up and grinned, but kept playing. Abe gazed down at his drum. Peter stood up and stepped down off the patio.

"Who's in the house?"

Abe patted and whacked the drum loudly, and then stopped. Ben held his strings quiet.

"That's just our old man, man," Ben said. "The patriarch himself."

"Why doesn't he come out and join the party?" Maggie asked. Hers and Scott's eyes were just slits. Peter thought they definitely looked stoned.

"How many are here now?"

"Chill out, man. Take a seat. We're all right here."

"How many are in the house?"

"Peter, take it easy," Maggie said.

"Come on, guys, we should get back to the boat. Thanks for the weed, fellas. We've gotta hit the road."

"But I don't want to go. It's so peaceful here. Come on, Peter. Relax."

Peter looked to Scott for support, but Scott just grinned stupidly. "Yeah, man, we all just need to relax."

Peter watched Scott talk and then saw the cabin door open behind his two friends. A bone-thin man shuffled out and stood in the doorway. He had a long, white beard that grew down to his bare chest. His skin was covered with ugly crusted sores, just like his sons' skin. The only clothing he wore was a mud-covered pair of jeans, held up by a frayed rope. He was holding his hands behind his back.

Maggie and Scott leaned back to look up at him.

"Hey, mister, what instrument do you play?" Maggie asked.

The old man smiled wide to reveal a mouthful of rotten teeth. Peter took a step back. The man pulled an ax up behind Scott and, with a sudden violent motion, swung it with both hands down into his shoulder. Scott cried out, as a dark fountain of blood sprayed up over his head.

Ben sprung out of his chair, screaming, and smashed Scott across the face with the ukulele. Abe dove across the patio and pinned Maggie to the boards. Peter took two steps back and then spun around and ran. He heard Scott's muffled cry for help, and Maggie scream. He heard the old man howl, the two boys cackle, and the smash of the ax into Scott's body.

The demonic screams washed out his friends' shrieks for help.

The rain had stopped, and he ran as fast as he could, back down the trail, through the mud, and through the trees. Branches whipped his face and legs. Bushes cut through his skin. He cried and panted as he ran, back the way he came, through the darkness. After a few minutes, he stopped under a large tree trunk, gasping for air. He threw up.

"Oh fuck," he muttered. "Oh fuck oh fuck oh fuck." His eyes were wild. He spit, held his breath, and listened. Nothing but crickets. "Okay, okay. I need to get back to the boat. We push off. We go get the police."

He thought of Scott, dead in that cabin. He thought of Maggie, raped and murdered. Why didn't I help them? What could I have done? Oh fuck, oh fuck, they're going to find me. They're going to kill me. He closed his eyes and took a deep breath. I need to pull it together. I'm going to make it back to the boat. I'm going to make it back to the boat, and I'm going to go home, and I'm going back to Denver. I'll tell all my friends about this. The cops will put them all in jail. Oh fuck, they killed Scott! He stood up, pulled the knife out of the sheath, and held the flashlight in the other hand.

No. Fuck. I've got to go back. Fuck fuck fuck. Shit. Okay, Pedro, don't think, just do. He ran back toward the cabin, hyperventilating with fear. He saw the light from the cabin in front of him. As he approached, he saw two forms huddled over Scott.

"Get the fuck off him!" he screamed, the beam of his flashlight flailing wildly across the tree canopy. The heads shot up. They were the two brothers, but their faces made Peter stop dead in his tracks. Their mouths were drenched in blood. They were feasting on Scott's entrails. Their eyes were searing red, and their hair whipped around like snakes. Peter was trembling. He swung the flashlight directly at them.

"Get out of here!" he yelled. "Get out." He stepped forward, holding up his knife. "Where's my girlfriend!" He took another step. The two brothers paused their feast in the flash light beam, then dove back down and kept eating. Peter shouted incoherently and rushed them. He made it to the first step and lunged toward the nearest, slashing downward with his blade. The brother jumped out of the way with startling speed and shot straight up. Ben was still eating. Peter kicked him in the head. The kick threw Peter off balance and barely moved his target. He stumbled across the porch, dropping the flashlight. Abe was on him in a second, punching him in the back of the neck. Peter collapsed to the ground, and Abe jumped on his back. Peter spun around and sliced Abe across his stomach. Abe took a swing at Peter's face, clawing his ear, nose, and cheek. Peter blocked Abe's next punch and then jabbed straight up with his knife and caught Abe under the chin. Blood poured down out of Abe's throat and spilled over Peter's hand. He pulled out the knife and shoved him off. Abe collapsed to the wooden floorboards at the feet of Ben and the old man who had killed Scott. The old man was holding Maggie.

"You can back off right about now," the old man said, jostling Maggie by the arm. "Or you're gonna watch me gut this girl before my boys get you." Maggie was covered in blood, gasping between tears.

Peter scrambled up and took a few steps back. He held out the knife.

"Don't you fucking touch her. I'll kill your whole fucking family."

"Son," the old man said, "you are in no position to be making threats." As he spoke, Abe pulled himself up off the floor and wiped his chin. His eyes glowed. His snarling grin flashed his sharp teeth. Peter watched him get up, his mind not registering the impossible chaos unfolding.

"Give me the girl," Peter talked, instead of shouted. "We will leave, and we won't say anything. We won't come back. We won't report anything. Just let us go, okay?"

Ben and Abe both jumped at Peter at the same time.

"Run!" Maggie shrieked. She jerked her arm free from her captor, shoved him as hard as she could, knocking him back into the cabin. She leaped over Scott's carcass, cleared the stairs, and hit the ground running. Peter stabbed Ben in the arm as he attacked. Ben jerked back from Peter's knife and fell backward off the deck. Peter saw Maggie running out of the corner of his eye. He landed hard on the floor, and Abe fell back on top of him again. Peter thought he was dead. Then he realized Abe's body felt like dead weight. Peter pushed him off and scrambled back. Abe didn't move. Neither did Ben. And the old man was sprawled out facedown in the cabin. Peter jumped up, surging with adrenaline. He rolled Abe over with his foot. His features had changed back to when he had first seen him. He had red hair and white skin, like a person. The glow was gone from his eyes, and the same for his brother. Ben groaned feebly.

"Maggie!" Peter sprinted down the path toward her. "Maggie, wait!" He ran wildly in the dark, realizing he had forgotten his flashlight. His weapon felt reassuring in his hand. "Maggie!" he yelled again.

"Shh…" A whisper came from behind a thick cottonwood tree trunk. "Over here."

Peter rounded the tree to see Maggie crouched down between the roots. He squatted down at eye level to see her eyes in the darkness.

"Did they do anything to you?"

"Scott," she said, bewildered.

"Scott…Scott. Yeah. Yeah. We need to get out of here."

"Fuck, Peter," she sobbed. "They were going to kill you."

"We need to get out of here now. Are you ready to run?"

She nodded silently. He pulled her up and absentmindedly brushed off her shorts. "Don't stop until we get back to the boat, okay?"

She nodded in agreement. He turned and took off back down the trail.

22

After what seemed like half an hour, they still couldn't find the shore. Each time he thought he saw the shore, he just found more trees, more forest. He couldn't believe the island was this big. He realized they must have been going the wrong way. He slowed down and listened. He could only hear the crickets and his pounding heart. He decided to turn in the opposite direction and cut his way through the bushes and weeds, many as tall as him. Finally, he could see a clearing. He looked back to Maggie, signaling to wait, and pointed. She nodded in understanding and crouched down. He jumped out from the trees, expecting to see water. He didn't see water, just mud. It was about one hundred yards across—nothing but wet mud. Thick groves of trees lined the opening on all sides. He realized the moon was out. The clouds had dissipated, and he could see a little better. The stars and the moon cast a pale light on him as he stood on the edge of the mud field.

"What the fuck?" he whispered. He could make out a form jutting several feet out of the ground in the middle of the field. It looked man-made, like a stone well or an altar. He started to walk toward it, but then he saw something and froze: across the opening, movement. He jumped back into the trees and squatted down with Maggie, holding his breath.

A form materialized in the field. In the moonlight he could see one of the two brothers. He crouched lower and watched, grasping his knife as tight as he could, his hands and his whole body drenched in sweat. The brother, it looked like Ben, was sniffing, jerking his head back and forth as he slogged through the field. Suddenly a light shone from directly behind Peter. The beam shot over his back and past his head over the mud. Ben snapped his head and stared directly toward them.

"Maggie, turn off that…," Peter started. Maggie didn't have the flashlight. She was staring back at the source. Ben ran at them. The flashlight flipped off and Abe grabbed Maggie by the hair. Peter rushed to grab her, but Ben caught up to him first and struck him to the ground.

Ben kicked Peter in the ribs and then left him curled up on the ground. He grabbed Maggie by both arms. Abe let go of her hair and presented a machete. He cackled and pointed the machete at her face. He lifted her chin up with the blade and peered hungrily at her body. Ben thrust his pelvis into her behind, shaking her, while Abe gently played with the sword around her neck.

"Let her go, you motherfuckers!" Peter yelled as he staggered back up.

Abe spun around to face him and raised the machete. Ben pulled Maggie toward the middle of the clearing. Maggie struggled to escape. Peter stepped back as Abe approached. Ben reached the stone mound in the middle of the field and threw Maggie, headfirst, down onto the stone mound. She disappeared. Ben pulled two thin knives out of his pockets, and ran the two blades against each other. Abe attacked. Peter ducked his blow and then stabbed him in the stomach with his knife, all the way up to the hilt. Abe gasped and dropped his machete. Peter turned to block Ben's oncoming attack, still holding Abe by his knife handle. He pushed Abe into his brother, tearing out his knife and pushing them both down. He lunged on top of Abe, and swung widely with his bloody knife at Ben. Ben deflected the blows by rolling under his brother. He kneed Peter in the crotch, sending him hurtling over into the mud. They both jumped up and faced each other. Abe lay on the ground motionless.

"Not again," Ben croaked. His voice was shrill and evil. "You killed"—he started laughing all of a sudden—"my little bro. Twice today." He laughed.

Peter ran over and picked up the machete. Ben picked his knives up off the ground.

"You killed my friends! I'm going to kill you, you motherfucker!" Peter screamed, adrenaline coursing through his veins.

"Peter?" he heard Maggie all of a sudden. He glanced over at the pile of rocks. There was a black hole in the middle of it. It was a well. "Peter? Help me. Oh God, help me!"

"Maggie!" he shouted, darting his eyes back to Ben. Ben was standing up straight now, with his weapons dangling loosely in his hands. "Maggie, stay there. I'm coming for you."

Ben croaked with laughter, his voice now deep and raspy.

"Shut the fuck up. I'm going to kill you!" Peter yelled, and ran in for the attack. Ben ran up to meet him, knives out. The two collided, stabbing wildly at each other. Ben sliced through Peter's shoulder as Peter's knife found a place between Ben's ribs. Ben tried to stab him in the face, but Peter dodged. Then he felt a deep cut across his back. He stabbed with all his might into Ben's leg right above the knee, then jerked the knife out and jumped back. Ben held up his blood-covered knives and hands and grinned like a wolf. The dreadlocks on Ben's head writhed like snakes in the night air. Peter felt the blood running down his shoulder, but he couldn't feel any pain.

"You're all dead," Ben cackled. "You're all meat. Meat is murder!"

Peter's whole body shook uncontrollably. He could barely stand, chest heaving. "You're a cow. You're a pig." Ben pointed with one of his thin knives to the blood running down Peter's arm. "You're a fucking cheeseburger with ketchup, man! I'm gonna eat your tongue. Dad's gonna eat your liver. Abe's gonna eat your brains. And Ma's gonna eat your girlfriend!" He rubbed his stomach. "We've got the munchies!"

Then Abe stood up. The two brothers howled with laughter. Peter was frozen, shell-shocked.

"Peter!" Maggie's scream snapped him out of it.

He darted toward the well. The two hurtled after him, snarling and swinging. They caught up to him right as he reached the stone well. As he dove, a knife slashed through his shoe and caught his heel. He felt the deep cut as he plunged into darkness. He bashed his head against a wet jagged rock in midair, spun upside down, and then landed with a tremendous splash into the stagnant water below. He looked up to see two pairs of evil eyes peering down, their dreadlocks twisting in the moonlight. Then he blacked out.

23

Inside the houseboat, under the kitchen light, Gary held Karen and caressed her back. Mandy sat at the table across from Beth and Jen, and the three took turns swigging from the bottle of Jäger.

"That miserable pussy piece of shit. I can't believe he left me."

"Maybe he couldn't control the boat. He could still be trying to get back," Jen offered.

"No, he left. You don't know Joe. It's his goddamn temper. I swear to Christ, I'm going to chop his dick off in his sleep. You girls got any smokes?"

Beth reached in her bag and pulled out a pack of Marlboro Lights. She took three out and handed one each to Mandy and Jen. While she was fishing for a lighter, Jerrod stood over the table and offered a flame from his Zippo to Mandy.

Mandy leaned in to light up and then raised her eyes to meet Jerrod. "Thank you," she said, and then took a long drag. She exhaled, and then reached up, put her hand around the back of Jerrod's neck, and pulled him down close to her face. Beth and Jen watched intently as she stuck her tongue into Jerrod's mouth, making out with him deeply. She pulled back slowly.

"Oh my God," Jen said to Beth. Mandy turned slowly and peered at her across the table.

"Whoa, better hope Joe doesn't come back around—am I right, young man?" Gary asked, chuckling. Jerrod smiled at him and took a drag.

"Don't worry, kiddies." Mandy still stared at Jen. "We're grown-ups. This is what grown-ups do on vacation." She reached up and squeezed Jerrod's arm. "It's okay, baby. Joe's a big boy. He can handle it."

Karen joined Gary in the laughter. Jen and Beth looked at each other uncomfortably. Mandy caught the glance.

"What—are you telling me that hot little things like you don't swing?"

"Mandy May!" Karen exclaimed. Mandy waited for the girls' response.

"No," Jen said. Beth shook her head in agreement.

"Fuck yeah. I knew it!" Jerrod said. "I knew you were down the minute I saw you. Holy shit."

"Since when did you and Joe become swingers?" Karen asked, acting shocked.

"Oh, like you're Miss Goody Two-shoes all of a sudden. Must I remind you of that little trip to Nice?"

"Hey-oh!" Gary blurted out. "What do you say, kids. Want to pretend like we're all on the French Riviera? I'm wearing my Speedo!"

"Oh God, shut up. That's gross!" Jen said, pushing Beth out of the way and standing up. "Our friends are missing, you just crashed our boat, and you want to have what, an orgy?"

Jerrod and Gary both looked at each other, then back at the girls, and shrugged.

Mandy smirked.

"I'm going to bed," Jen said. She pulled a butter knife out of the kitchen drawer. "Anyone so much as sticks their nose in my room, and I'm gonna cut it off. Got it!"

"Take it easy, honey," Mandy purred. "You don't have to play if you don't want to. It's just that I'm a little stressed and a little drunk, and I think it would be nice to take my mind off things for a while. What's so wrong with that?" She turned to look at Beth.

"Nothing," Beth said. "Do whatever you want. It's a free country."

"Beth, are you coming to bed?" Jen demanded.

"I'm not drunk enough to go to bed yet," Beth replied, taking another sip.

Jen snorted, spun around, and marched into one of the bedroom compartments, butter knife in hand.

"Come on, honey." Karen tugged at Gary's arm. "I think you've had enough excitement for one day. You kids mind if we take one of the bunks?"

Jerrod and Beth both nodded. Gary looked crestfallen, and sauntered behind his wife as she led him away. "Mandy, behave yourself," she said as they withdrew to bed.

"Well, you too." Mandy put out her cigarette. "What do you feel like doing?" Jerrod breathed in to say something, but Mandy reached across the table and put her hand on his crotch. Whatever he was going to say, he stopped. Beth stood in the kitchen, watching. Mandy stood up, pulled Beth over, until their three bodies were pressed against each other, and then kissed Beth fully on the lips. Beth slowly caressed her breasts. Jerrod watched the two and inhaled their scents. Mandy stroked him through his swimsuit with one hand and held Beth by the small of her back with the other. She turned and made out with Jerrod, while Beth lifted up her tank top and sucked on one of her nipples.

Mandy sighed lustfully. "Who wants to play with Mommy?"

Beth pulled Mandy's face back over and licked her lips and teeth. Mandy stepped away and lead them both by the hands back to the last vacant bedroom. She told Jerrod to get undressed and then untied Beth's bikini top and tossed it on the floor. Jerrod sat on the bed, touching himself and watching as Mandy sat back against his leg, pulling Beth down to her. She licked Beth's small pink nipples. Beth moaned while she ran her fingers through Mandy's hair. Jerrod cupped Mandy's large breast and then pulled her by the shoulder down to him. Mandy rolled over to one side of Jerrod, and Beth lay down on the other side. She started kissing his chest as Mandy slid down and parted her lips over his cock.

"Ahhh, Jesus!" He came instantly. "Oh God." Jerrod's eyes rolled back in his head. He lifted his head up to look at both of them. "Sorry."

"Don't worry, baby," Mandy giggled. "We'll come back to you in a minute." Beth lunged across Jerrod's pelvis, kissing her forcefully. The two rolled over, pushing Jerrod out of the way. He stared in embarrassed amazement as the women went to town.

Gary was passed out on his back, snoring loudly. Karen couldn't sleep, listening between her husband's snores to the sounds of her best friend since college fucking two kids who probably were in college. She tossed and turned and finally got up to go to the bathroom. She got out of bed naked, slipped on her shorts and t-shirt, pushed back the curtain, and tiptoed into the hall. Mandy was squealing and breathing heavy. Karen shook her head and felt her way down the hall to the bathroom. She flipped on the light, looked in the tiny shower, then in the toilet, and then looked at herself in the mirror. She rubbed her eyes, sighed, and then pulled her shorts down and sat on the pot. She peed, and as she wiped herself, she heard moans again. But it didn't sound like Mandy.

She paused motionless and listened. Well, it was probably one of the kids. She tiptoed up to the bathroom door and stuck her ear against the crack. She couldn't hear anything now, not even Gary's snores. After a few moments, she heard giggling from the ménage à trois, so she opened the door and walked back to her room. She undressed in the dark, pulled back the covers, and slid into bed. She rolled over and laid her arm across Gary's chest. It was wet. She patted him. She sniffed her fingers and then licked her fingertip.

"Gary?" She shook him. "Gary?" She jumped up and turned on the light. "Oh, no, no!" she wailed.

Gary was a lifeless pile of pulp. His body was covered with blood. His face was reduced to a bloody skull. Pools of blood spilled out of his eye sockets. His cheeks and lips were completely gone. His chest was covered in deep wounds, and his stomach hung over the bed like a disgusting web of snakes and worms. She ran screaming out into the hall. Jerrod exploded out of the room naked. Mandy and Beth followed behind. Karen crashed into Jerrod, her hand splattering blood across him. "He's dead! He's dead," she sobbed. Mandy reached for her and held her as she convulsed. Jerrod ran into the bedroom and threw up at the sight.

"Fuck!" he shouted, clutching his hair in his fists. "Fuck!"

"This just happened! I was just there a minute ago!"

"Did you see anyone?" Maggie tried to get her attention, but she was in hysterics. "Did you see anyone, Karen?"

"Okay, shut up, shut up!" Jerrod yelled. "Beth, go back to the room. Mandy, take her with you, and go with Beth. Jen, you okay?" No answer. "Jen!"

He ran into Jen's room. Empty. "Jen!" he yelled, tearing through the kitchen. He ran outside onto the deck. It had stopped raining, but he didn't notice. "Jen!" he screamed, and then ran back through to the other end of the boat. He ran out onto the back then flew up the spiral staircase. "Jen, answer me!" he choked, sobbing and spitting out the words. Nothing came back. Then screams came from down in the boat. He spun back around and hurtled down the stairs. Ripping open the bedroom curtain, he saw Karen slumped face-down on the bed. "Where are they!" he shouted, flipping her over. She was dead. A giant bloody wound started at her neck and traveled all the way down to between her legs. Her head rolled back to reveal her throat was torn out. He thought he was going to pass out.

Propping himself up by the wall, he looked to see a flash of movement out on the front deck. He ran toward it, and thought he could see Mandy's blond hair in the darkness. He burst onto the deck, took a running leap onto the shore, and chased after them into the night. He saw movement in the trees and followed. Rocks tore through his bare feet, and barbs ripped through his exposed skin. He ran as fast as he could, ignoring the searing pain. He ran, and his mind blazed with fear and hatred. He ran and cursed and screamed like a maniac. Suddenly he tripped over something and crashed to the ground. He choked, gasping for air. He jumped back up and then stopped. At his feet, gazing up at him, with big red lips wide open, was Mandy's head.

24

Peter opened his eyes and couldn't remember where he was. It was dark, but he thought he could see a light far in the distance. He felt around on the ground. He could feel wet, loose gravel and dirt. He tried to stand up, but his legs buckled, and he immediately fell back to the ground. He fumbled over to a rock wall and pulled himself up. Staggering against the wall, he slowly made his way toward the light. He felt sick to his stomach as the events of the evening came back to him. He paused, and then took another step into a void. He plummeted off a ledge into water. He thrashed around, gasping for air.

"Relax, Peter," Maggie's voice came from nearby. He stopped at the sound of her voice and realized his feet could touch bottom. He stood up.

"Maggie? Where are you?"

"I'm right here," she said. He saw her hand and arm come out of the darkness, and then he saw her face. "Come on, let me help you up." He held her hand, and she pulled him back up on the ledge. He collapsed at her feet, pulling her down and holding her close. The two sat huddled in the darkness, shivering.

He woke up, again not sure where he was. He felt Maggie's warmth and remembered.

"How long was I out?"

"Only a few minutes."

"Where are we?"

"I don't know."

"Are you okay?" he asked.

She didn't reply.

"Scott," he said. She hushed him and hugged him tight.

"Don't talk, Peter. We need to listen."

He looked into her eyes, welling with tears.

"We need to listen, Peter," she whispered. "For when they come to get us."

"I won't let that happen."

"Shhh. Listen."

He listened. All he could hear was their breathing.

"We should keep moving," he mouthed, almost silently. "That way."

They slowly rose together, carefully lowered themselves into the water, and started wading up the tunnel. Peter kept looking back but only saw darkness. As they pressed forward, they began to be able to make things out in the darkness. Most looked like fish bones of all shapes and sizes, piled on top of each other on the sides. Some of the bones looked impossibly huge: a spine five feet long, then a jaw bone that could have been as big as a whale's. Black bones leaned against the passage walls, some almost to the ceiling. Decaying fish skulls peered back at them like watchful guards. Faded cracks twisted in the rocks walls, forming patterns. Spirals cut into the slick stones, and crude carvings depicted small bodies piled under giant menacing faces. Peter leaned in closer to see a jagged evil face spewing legs and arms and heads from its gaping maw. Hundreds of sharp tiny bones piled up out of the water on either side of their path. The piles grew bigger until they cracked underfoot, and they had to push them aside like they were in a swamp of death. The smell was unbearable.

Something grazed his leg. He kicked and lurched around.

"I just felt something!" He frantically looked to see any movement.

Maggie grabbed a pile of bones off the ledge on her side and pulled herself up out of the water.

"Over there!" She pointed.

Peter turned but didn't see anything. He grabbed a hammer-size bone out of the water and shook with fear.

"It's just a fish. These are all fish bones, right? This is just a river, right?"

"Peter, get up here with me."

"This is just fucking Illinois, and Scott didn't just get fucking killed, right!" he screamed.

"Peter! Get up here now!"

Peter was hit from behind on both legs with a force that knocked him back into the water. He flayed wildly, batting at the black water with his weapon. A sickening pain ripped through his thigh, and he screamed.

25

"No, leave him alone!" Maggie shouted.

Peter saw massive forms break the surface of the water around him, dive back below, and a sharp tail sliced across his arm. He grasped his leg and felt holes in his skin. Something clamped down on his other calf, and then horrible pain erupted. This time it didn't let go but pulled him under. He let go of the bone and punched wildly in the water. He made contact, and when his fist hit scales, his fear turned to rage. A thing bit down harder on his leg as he pounded, hitting as hard as he could. He kicked the top of its head. It was shaking him furiously, dragging him back down. He planted his foot and pushed up. Gasping for air, he dove once again, grabbed the thing by its tail with both hands, and heaved with all of his strength. The tail slipped out of his hands. He was dizzy and frantic. It loosened its bite momentarily. Peter slipped away. It attacked again. This time Peter hit it in the face, jabbing it on the nose. He thrashed around him, stood up, wild-eyed, and teetered backward. The water was still.

"Oh Jesus, Peter. Are you okay?" Maggie said from her perch.

Peter didn't answer, seized by shock. He stood there in the middle of the water passage.

"Fuck me," he finally said, pulling himself back up on the ledge. He was soaked with filth, and his leg stung where he'd been bitten. He collapsed in Maggie's arms, and they both fell in a huddled mass on the slime-covered stone.

They embraced in the dark silence. Maggie rocked Peter, and he squeezed her as tight as he could. "I need to get a weapon," he panted. "A gun."

"We need to call the police," she said back.

He stood and lifted her up by her hands. He started down the corridor, running his fingers over the tunnel wall, and shuffling through the fish bones. Maggie followed, straining to see any sign of light in the passage. They walked for what seemed like hours. The bones kept tripping them as they stumbled forward, but eventually the waterway diverted into the opposite wall of the tunnel. The exhausted pair kept on marching through rotten bones, the stench growing unbearable. They slowly realized they could make out more features of their surroundings, without any discernible light source.

"Peter," Maggie said, too calmly.

He stopped and turned back to look. She was staring at the stone wall, wild-eyed. He limped over and squinted to see. As he realized what he was looking at, his heart started pounding through his chest.

26

The two stood at the wall, staring at carvings in the rock face. Countless ancient hieroglyphics had been cut into the rock from the floor up out of sight. Peter followed Maggie's stare to an image of a horrible face, mouth gaping open, and people pouring into the mouth. The carving depicted women and children being eaten alive, body parts hanging between massive teeth. Carnage spilled from the lips, and massive mounds of bodies piled beneath. Tiny people swirled around the devouring god. The image continued as they walked—thousands of people bowing down, worshipping the deity. Mixed in with the people were images of fire and smoke. Trees, fields, people on fire. The mural went on as they walked. A pyramid emerged, with another demon god feasting on human flesh at the top. Hundreds of people below lifted their hands up in praise as they were showered with blood.

Peter was thinking that the god's face looked kind of catfish-like, when they heard a noise. He grabbed

Maggie's arm, and they crouched down by the floor. A light started to glow far down the tunnel, and now they heard something again. Voices. Many voices.

"What should we do?" Maggie asked.

"Shh…listen," Peter said, barely able to hear over his pounding heart. The voices grew louder. They were calling out a name.

"Are they saying, 'Shannon'?" He listened again, they were closer now. "Shannon Greene. Shannon?"

"Oh shit," Maggie said, clutching Peter's arm. "Shannon Greene?"

"You know her?"

"Yeah, I do. Look." Distracted, Peter looked down to see what Maggie was holding. It was her fake ID.

"Oh, fuck. You're Shannon Greene. They're looking for you!"

"We're saved!" She jumped up.

"No, wait—" Peter started.

"Come on, they're looking for us," she cried. "We're safe." Maggie started running toward the voices, and Peter followed. The light grew brighter, and the voices grew louder. The tunnel seemed to ascend. They turned a corner, and moving toward them were a dozen or more beams of light.

"Shannon Greene. Thank good God almighty," said a man. "You doing all right, young lady?"

"Who's there?" Maggie asked.

"Don't worry, ma'am, this is Bill Franks, from the marina—Mac's Marina. We heard some of you were lost."

"Oh, thank God," Maggie said. "We need help," she said, shivering in the flashlight beam.

Peter stepped forward. "Our friend was just killed—murdered. We aren't all right," he said.

Bill shone the light in his eyes. "I'm sorry to hear that, son. We've got the authorities out looking for a few of you tonight. The Bains are missing someone too."

"Why are you all down here?" Maggie asked.

"To find you, Maggie," a different voice said. She froze.

"Who said that?" Peter asked immediately. "Get those fucking flashlights out of my face."

The flashlights stayed trained, right in their eyes, for ten seconds, and then one dropped off.

"Maggie, it's me," a man said. A light shone from below his face, casting a grotesque shadow up onto the ceiling of the tunnel. A wispy beard ran along his jawline. A pointed goatee covered his chin. His long hair was pulled back into a ponytail. Peter had never seen him before. He felt Maggie dig her nails into his skin as she squeezed his forearm.

"Jacob?" she gasped.

27

The two stood in silence, Maggie holding Peter's arm. Then she let go and walked toward the man's glowing face.

"Jacob? What are you doing here?"

"I wanted to help find you. You went missing. Come here, babe. You're safe now."

"How did you know her name?" Peter muttered under his breath. No answer. "How do you know her name?" he asked again.

Jacob's light swung off his face and shone back into Peter's eyes. "So this is the boyfriend?" he asked.

Some of the people holding flashlights shuffled forward. Maggie and Peter took a step back in unison.

"Maggie, how does this guy know your name?" Peter asked.

"Peter,"—Maggie swallowed—"this is Jacob, a friend. Peter, Jacob. Jacob, Peter."

"Get that fucking flashlight out of my fucking face!" Peter yelled. "Jacob…Bill…whoever the fuck you are—can you give us some water or blankets or a goddamn way out of this fucking nightmare?"

"Jacob, it's really freaky that you are down here right now. Can you please tell me what's going on?"

"You weren't supposed to come down here Maggs. I'm here to take you back to your friends."

"Our friend just got murdered," Peter said. "Murdered!"

As he yelled, Peter felt a tug at his shirt. He put his face an inch away from Maggie's in the light. She glanced down. He followed her glance. She handed him something. It felt heavy in his hand. A big chunk of rock. He looked back up. Maggie was visibly trembling.

"So, I'm confused," said Bill's voice. "Is one of them Shannon, and the other is Maggie? Or is that one of them's full name, or what?"

"No," said Jacob. "Her name is Maggie Dymerski, and his name is Peter Rockwood."

"Oh, so Shannon Greene is not her real name?" Bill asked.

"No," Jacob said, "it's the name on her fake ID she gave you to rent your boat."

"Fake ID? Now, why would she do a thing like that?"

"Because she's not old enough to rent a houseboat, Bill."

"Ohhh. So they used a fake ID to steal a boat from me? To steal from me?" His voice grew an octave higher.

"No," Maggie said, "we weren't stealing." Her voice rattled with adrenaline. "We are returning the boat, just like we agreed to. We paid with a credit card. It's paid for."

"Now listen, guys," Peter said. "None of this matters. Fake ID, boat, whatever. Did you not just hear me tell you that our friend was just killed in front of our own eyes, not an hour ago? The killers could be anywhere. They killed him with a fucking ax. Can we please get out of here, go back to town, go to the police, and straighten all this out?" Silence. "Let's go get the bad guys?"

"Maggie, what do you see in this guy? What a whiner."

"Shut up, Jacob."

"How the fuck does he know about you and me? How does he know my name?"

"Wow, real genius. Peter, Maggie and I have been spending a lot of quality time together lately if you know what I mean."

"Shut the fuck up, Jacob," she said. The group grew closer, and Maggie took another step back.

"Sorry, Maggie," Peter whispered. "I'm real fucking sorry for everything." Then he stepped in front of her and threw the rock as hard as he could, aiming for Jacob. The rock sailed past Jacob and hit someone's shin. The corridor exploded with shouts as the group ran at the pair.

Maggie threw another rock. Peter bent down to feel for anything, and his hand came over a long bone. He smashed it in two, creating a sharp, jagged edge. The crowd was on him. He swung fiercely, blindly, and connected with the first attacker. The flashlight dropped to the ground and spun, revealing the hoard of people descending upon them. Peter went wild with rage and fear, slashing and stabbing with his weapon. Someone big came at him. He blocked a blow with his elbow and then stabbed him in the chest.

Maggie had rolled to the floor to avoid the first assault and then sprang up in the middle of the group and started kicking. She kicked one in the small of the back, then another in the face, then swiped a guy across the face, tearing his cheek and nose. She thrashed out at everyone who came within arm's length, until there were too many of them.

One tackled her from behind, then two more grabbed her legs. They pinned her down to the ground, and another lay across her stomach. She screamed with terror. A man grabbed the bone out of Peter's hand and knocked him over the head with it. Peter held up his hands feebly to defend himself, but then dizziness overcame him, and he collapsed to the ground. Out of one eye, he could see Maggie still struggling.

Peter coughed. He tasted blood in his mouth. Then something was in between him and Maggie. Two feet walked up to his face. Birkenstocks. Jacob leaned down so he was almost eye level with Peter.

"Total bummer, dude," Jacob said.

"Fuck you," Peter wheezed, "you goddamn dirty hippie."

"Hahaw!" Jacob laughed. "Now that's just some typical close-minded Midwestern redneck talk right there."

Peter glared up at Jacob.

"I'm going to fuck—" Peter started to say, until Jacob squared off and kicked him in the face. Blood splattered out of Peter's mouth. Maggie screamed.

"All right, all right. Everyone just settle down," Bill's voice boomed through the tunnel. "Boys, you got that lady under control?" A half dozen yeses echoed through the chamber. "Jacob, need any help?"

"Yeah," he said. "Help me get this sad sack of crap up on his feet."

A few more came over and lifted Peter up. Then they pulled Maggie up. The two stood, surrounded by the breathing of the attackers. Then the attackers tied their arms behind their backs.

"All right, folks," Bill said, "let's do it."

With that, the two were led down the tunnel.

28

They marched in silence. Maggie's mind was exploding with pain and wonder. Why was Jacob here? Why did he kick Peter? How did these people get down here? Her mind snapped back to her steps as a hand grabbed her shoulder roughly.

"Keep moving," someone barked, pushing her forward.

"Where are you taking us?" Peter asked. "Bill? Are you taking us to the police? If this is about the fake, we can take care of that—no problem."

"The police have been notified and are already on the scene," someone else said from behind.

As they continued around a bend, they saw light coming from a light bulb ahead.

"Have they caught the murderers? I can identify them in a lineup or whatever," Peter said. "We can help."

"No need. I think we've got it under control."

Peter stopped in his tracks and turned around. It was the same pie-faced cop from Utica.

"Turn around and shut up," he said, jabbing Peter in the gut. Peter curled up in pain, and then the cop spun him around and pushed him forward. Peter took two steps and then fell to the ground. "Get up, boy!" the cop said. "Get up and march, soldier!" Peter slowly got up and started walking again. This isn't good, he thought. A cop. The marina guy. What the hell are they doing? This is it. This is the end. No, wait. Don't think that. You can't think that. You're going to make it. You're going back to see your mom and dad. You're going back to ski. White snow. You're going to be back in your tent with Maggie. Maggie. Naked in the field of sunflowers with Maggie. The hot sun and your sweat and melted ice cream. Maggie's face and lips and skin on you and under you, and her cold tongue sharing ice cream with yours. Maggie knows Jacob. Maggie knows Jacob? Oh, fuck it.

"Maggie?" Peter said looking down.

"Shut up!" the cop said.

"How do you know Jacob?"

"Shut up, boy!" the cop nearly screamed.

"No, it's all right," Jacob said. "We're nearly there anyway. I could use a break."

"What time is it?" Bill asked in his singsong voice.

"Why, I think it's just about four twenty," Jacob said. He checked his wrist where there wasn't any watch. "Yep, sure is. Four twenty, man!"

"What the fuck," Maggie said. "Why do you have me tied up, Jacob? What are you doing?"

"Like you need to ask, Maggs," he laughed, sitting down cross-legged. "Take a seat."

Peter stayed standing until the cop pushed him down, hard.

Maggie kneeled down. "Jacob, you have to listen to me," she said, staring into his eyes. "How do you know these people? Why do you have me tied up?"

"Hey, man, if it was up to me, I'd have you untied immediately. But these other folks don't know you as well as I know you. And you did attack us after all. Pete here threw a rock at me. That's just not cool, man." He pulled a Ziploc bag from his pocket and unrolled it to reveal a bag of weed.

Peter glanced over at the cop but got no reaction. Peter looked the other way, then over his shoulder. They were with a dozen people—all men. He recognized Bill, the cop, and a couple others that looked familiar. He realized Richard, the fat ass from the marina, was there too. So you were the one who got a hold of my bone knife. You fat fuck.

Most of them sat down in the middle of the dimly lit passage. Bill wandered ahead a little, looking around. Jacob rolled a joint, lit it, inhaled, closed his eyes, and then exhaled a large white cloud of smoke into Maggie's face. She coughed, and her eyes watered. Jacob passed the joint to a fifty-something-year-old guy next to him. The guy had his t-shirt tucked into his shorts and was wearing tennis shoes with socks pulled up to his knees. Jacob stared at Maggie, and Maggie stared back without breaking her gaze.

"Maggie and I have been kind of a thing since Christmas," Jacob said.

"That's not true."

"You see, Pete, after you headed west, Maggie and I met at a raging house party. Should have been there. Killer tunes, killer bud, killer babes."

Maggie glared silently.

He continued, "You know Matt…uh…Duman, right? Year or two older than you probably? Yeah, well, Matt knows some dudes, and I know some dudes, and those dudes had some hot senoritas coming over. And I just happened to have access to some freaking epic kush. So there I am in good ol' Dixon, Illinois, at some rich kid's parents' mansion. Parents gone. One hundred, maybe two hundred kids, just partying like 1999, you know." He laughed. "And that's where I met Maggs here. And the rest, as they say, man, is history. She is so hot when she's stoned."

"Where are you taking us?" Maggie snapped.

"Mellow out, dude. Are you cashed? You want a hit of this going around?"

"Where are you taking us?" she asked again.

"To the party," Jacob said.

"What party?" Peter asked.

Jacob sneered at him and didn't answer. Instead, he looked at Maggie.

"Do I need to be frightened right now?" she asked.

He shrugged.

"Do you know who killed Scott Hey?"

"That's enough, Jacob," Bill said as he walked back into the group. "Give me a hit of that funny stuff and let's hit the high road. We wait too much longer, and we're all in the doghouse."

"Don't want to keep the women waiting," fat Richard said.

The tunnel sloped uphill. Peter and Maggie trudged on, surrounded by their captors. Bill and Jacob were in the lead. The lights grew brighter, and the wet stone cavern made way to dry cement slabs. Finally they came to the foot of some stairs. They walked up. Bill unlocked a metal door at the top of the stairs, and they all walked out into Mac's Marina on the Illinois River, near Utica, Illinois, USA, planet Earth.

29

Maggie was beyond surprised. Her weed hookup had now taken her and her boyfriend hostage, with the help of, what appeared to be, half the men of Utica. Rude. She was too shell-shocked to be frightened. They haven't killed us yet. Maybe they are protecting us from the crazy hippies who killed Scott. But Jacob is kind of a hippie...No, that doesn't matter. There are tons of hippies out in the world, and a ton in Illinois. Peaceful, fun-loving hippies. Devil sticks and drum circles. Dancing Bears and LSD. Yes, he was worried about me, and he hates Peter, obviously. Jealousy maybe? She had told Jacob some pretty nasty things about Peter—one time in particular when she was lying in bed naked with Jacob, smoking a joint. Well, who knew they would ever meet? What the fuck are we doing back in this Marina?

"What the fuck are we doing back in this Marina?" Peter's voice broke the silence.

Maggie looked wide-eyed at him, wondering if he had read her mind.

"Shhh. Shut up time," the cop said. He jabbed Peter in the back and then pushed him out the door. The group filed out of the marina and around the harbor in the moonlight to the one houseboat left in the dock. The moon shone on the face of the black water. A light from the boat revealed people inside—many people. They were dressed in white.

"Permission to come aboard," said Bill.

"Permission granted," chanted a chorus of women's voices. "Come aboard."

Bill and Jacob walked onto the boat first, and then Peter and Maggie were pushed over the bow. They were forced to sit, and then Bill and a couple other men tied their ankles together.

"Davis, Richard, keep an eye on these two," Bill said.

Davis stood up tall and straightened his shorts. Richard wheezed and sweated in the thick summer air.

"Rest of you, inside."

They opened the cabin door to a wave of music and laughter and perfume. Peter strained to look and saw women dressed in white robes dancing and hugging the men as they entered the houseboat.

"Keep your eyes forward," said Richard.

"Hey, Richard," said Peter.

"Hey what?"

"Why don't you go choke on a donut, you fat piece of shit."

"That's hurtful."

"Untie us, and I'll show you something really hurtful."

"That would be dumb of me, now wouldn't it?"

"Why can't you just let me go," Maggie asked. "Maybe I've got something you want."

"No can do." He blushed. "Davis here would kill me if I let you go."

"Really? Davis, you would kill him if he let me go?"

"Yep."

"Well, why don't you both just go inside like the rest of your friends, and let us slip off into the night. We won't tell anyone anything. Our car is right over in that parking lot. We'll just leave."

"Too late for that," said Davis. "We're taking off."

The singing and music grew louder from inside the boat. The engine started up. Davis untied the ropes tethered to the dock and gave the thumbs-up to Bill, who was steering from inside. The boat pulled back out of the harbor and slowly made for open water. Maggie watched her car and the parking lot fall away in the night as they drifted out into the river.

"Well then, at least tell us where we are going," Maggie said.

Richard looked up at Davis and then back at the two. Davis shrugged and turned his back to them and started whistling.

"Okay, fair enough," Richard said. "You are going to see the queen."

"What queen?" Peter asked.

"Our queen. The queen who rules this land. The queen who gives us food and water and fish and meat and fruit and milk and women."

"And weed," Davis added.

"And weed," Richard said. "Holy smoke, you know. Royal smoke."

"Royal crock o' shit," Peter said. "You won't let us go. You won't tell us what the fuck is going on with the toga party back there. You tell us about some queen like we're all floating down the Thames. I can't believe I'm sitting here, tied up, listening to these words come out of your fat fucking mouth." As he spoke he could see inside the cabin in the reflection off Richard's thick glasses. Bill was no longer at the wheel. Well, this is as good a time to go as any, he thought.

"I'm going to kill you."

"Now here you go again," Richard said.

"I'm going to kill you!" Peter shouted at the top of his lungs. "Cocksucker motherfucker!" he screamed like a banshee, pulling his arms apart with all his might. With a rage that came deep from within, he snapped the bonds around his wrists and kicked his legs free at the same time.

He lunged across the bow at Richard and grabbed on to his neck with both hands. His fingers got lost in the thick folds of fat as he choked his throat. Davis spun around, his eyes glowing red. He looked completely different than just a moment before. He jumped at Peter, but Maggie lifted up her feet and tripped him. He fell facedown and started convulsing on the boat. Maggie lifted her legs up high like she used to in cheerleading, then swung them down as hard as she could on Davis' neck. A sickening cracking noise came from her blow, and she swung again with her heels, down again on the neck. Davis thrashed and

screamed, and Maggie kept kicking. Peter was straddled across Richard's fat chest and was doing his best
to choke him to death. Richard tried rolling over, but
Peter scurried out of the way of his massive frame and
still held on to his neck. Richard's eyes rolled back in
his head, and his tongue fell out of his mouth.

"Untie me," Maggie panted. "I think I just killed
this guy."

Peter looked. Sure enough, Davis wasn't moving.
Richard was still breathing. His massive gut lifted
up and down unnaturally, but he didn't seem to be
conscious. Peter checked the window. No one at the
cockpit, no one up front. They must all be in back. He
stooped down and untied Maggie's arms and feet.

She tried to stand and then fell into him. He looked
down. Davis had reached up and grabbed her ankle.
He looked up at her with an evil grimace, his head contorted to one side, his face covered in blood. Maggie
kicked him in the face and screamed. He howled and
thrashed his arms up at her.

Peter grabbed him by his tan tennis shoes and
pulled him to the tip of the bow. The shoes slipped
off, and Davis started scrambling across the deck again
toward Maggie. Peter rushed up just as Davis reached
her, grabbed him by the socks, and pulled him back
again. He looked around, but there was nothing to
bash Davis with.

Davis was clawing frantically, making guttural noises
that didn't sound human. Richard was starting to come
to, groaning. Peter lifted Davis up off the boat and
threw him overboard. Davis grabbed onto the rail with
one hand as he went over, and his body thudded against

the side of the boat. Maggie ran up and punched his knuckles, but he kept holding on, howling. He swung up to get a grip with the other hand, but Peter fought him off, batting his hand away each time. Maggie pried off Davis's thumb, then index finger, followed by his middle finger. He was now holding on by two fingers, screaming and punching into the air, kicking the water. His face was contorted like a demon, eyes wild and bloodred in the moonlight. She pulled away the ring finger.

"Do it for Christ sake!" Peter yelled.

She looked down.

Davis grew still all of a sudden and grinned. "You're all going to die," he said. "Axulche will feast on your insides tonight."

Maggie smashed his little finger with her fist, and Davis fell under the boat.

30

Jacob, Officer Tim O'Hara, and the rest of the men joined their brides out on the stern of the house-boat, toasting the monumental occasion and recounting the night's events. Lawrence Welk crooned "Moon River" from inside the boat.

"Here's to Jacob," Tim said, raising a glass of blood red wine, "for successfully delivering exactly what we needed for such an important event."

They all clinked glasses together and drank deeply.

"As promised," Jacob said, swirling his glass.

"And here's to Ben and Abe, and Joseph, too," said the woman standing next to Tim. "May they find the rest of our little friends and bring them in as quickly and quietly as Jacob here."

"Here, here!" Jacob said.

They clinked glasses again. But this time, the boat lurched. The wine sloshed out of glasses and onto several white robes.

"Ah, shoot. We musta hit a snag," Tim said. He and a few of the guys stuck their heads out to see what was making the engine sound funny. The boat lurched again, and the engine sounded like it would explode. They leaned out farther.

"Bill!" Jacob shouted. "Kill the engine!" Then he turned to the group surrounding him. "Someone shine a light down on that propeller."

Right as the light switched on, a mass of human flesh and gore exploded up from the engine and fanned out into the night. The propeller chopped through Davis's carcass, sending up chunks of fat and bone and spraying blood over the water. The blades cut the body in half, and an arm got wedged between the prop and the hull. The engine slowed, started to smoke, and then a severed hand shot straight up and fell back down across an old woman's face, like a pimp slap.

"Ha!" the woman next to her laughed. "I've got to hand it to you, Esther."

Esther looked down at the bloody palm and her bare feet, and then took a gulp of her wine. She tossed the empty glass overboard, lifted her arms up in the air, and started dancing. The other women joined in, dancing and cackling in the moonlight as blood continued to spray up out of the engine.

The remains of Davis floated behind them in pieces, some fifty yards apart, bobbing in the small wake.

Jacob ran back into the cabin, with Tim close behind. Bill wasn't at the wheel. "Bill!" Tim yelled. "We've got a problem!"

"I can see that," Bill replied from out on the bow.

"Where were you?" Jacob and Tim rushed out to join him. The kid, the girl, and Davis were gone. Bill was crouched over Richard like he was ready to pounce.

"I was in the head, if you want to know. Nature calls."

"Who was driving the boat?" Tim asked.

"I'm asking the questions now," Bill said with a snarl. "Now, Richard,"—he slapped Richard's fat cheek lightly with his knuckles—"I've got to ask you again, what happened?" Richard groaned, eyes still rolled up in his head. Bill leaned over so his mouth was inches from Richard's ear. "I'm only gonna ask you once more, private. Where'd the meat go?"

"He choked me," Richard gagged back.

"And where did they go after he choked you?"

"Don't know," he barely said.

"Okay. Thanks, big guy. You relax now. You need some water?"

The engine screamed again, then whirred and chopped as hot, fat, and stinking blood arched even higher in the air and a fresh body floated into the pro-peller. The scream wasn't the engine. It was Richard. He was alive, but only as long as the propeller took to chop off his foot, then knee, legs, scrotum, and stom-ach. He drowned, screaming, as the propeller tore through his intestines and twisted them into flying projectiles. The dancing women laughed vigorously with renewed glee. They put their hands on their part-ners' hips and swayed to the ancient dance, breathing the blood mist deeply into their nostrils.

"Axulche," one of them purred.

"Axulche!" the rest of the women chanted.

"Axulche," the men whispered desperately.

"Two have fallen. More will fall. All shall live."

"More will fall. All shall live."

"Axulche!" they all screamed in unison. "Axulche! Soet! Cuthsmx!"

31

"Well, shoot!" said Bill, standing up. "This isn't gonna work."

"What are we going to do?" Jacob asked.

"They can't get very far. We're just about across from you-know-where."

"And there's no way they can float back to the marina."

"Because it's upstream."

"Guess we better let the bros know." Bill walked back in and turned the vessel toward the island. Jacob stayed out on the bow, peering into the night. When the boat reached the shore, Bill and Jacob dropped down into the trees without saying a word to anyone. In back, the old people were taking off their clothes, getting naked, and wading out into the river. One by one, they each slithered off the boat and swam out into the darkness, toward the floating tissue and human blood on the water's surface.

Maggie and Peter spied over the top of the boat. Up on the roof, they lay and watched the strange night swimmers. After the entire party had swum out of sight, the two snuck down the ladder, down the side of the boat, then onto the sandy shore, and quickly stole into the trees.

"Well, what are we dealing with, Maggie?" Peter said as they walked.

"Would you be referring to the old man that turned into a crazy person and said something was going to eat us?" she asked quietly. "Or the ax-wielding maniac who killed Scott Hey, our starting quarterback? Or would you be referring to the nice little blood dance with the bridge club down below?"

"So, what's the deal with you and Jacob?"

"Are you serious," she scolded him. "Now you ask me about Jacob?"

"Yeah. So Jacob is why you want to see other people?"

"No. Jesus Christ. You are why I want to see other people. I love you." She kissed him fully, taking him and herself by surprise. "And I hate you." She sat back. "In case you've already forgotten, I just killed someone. Yes, they probably want to do the same to us. But nevertheless, I just pried that old man's pinky off so he could go through the old engine back behind this little boat."

"Yeah, I saw. Good job. Now we've got about twenty more to do that to, from what I can tell. And then we should be able to get the rest of the gang and get the fuck out of Dodge. So, until we do that, I want to know what the fuck is up with Jacob."

"I bought weed from him. We screwed a couple times. You happy? I was bored. I was high. I don't know. You didn't come back for Christmas break. I did. I haven't seen him since then. I've seen other guys back at school since then. He's nothing, but…"

"But what?" Peter asked. Maggie was silent. "But what?"

Her eyes grew bigger. "Nothing," Maggie said. "It's nothing."

"What is it? Come on. I know you better than that. What is it?"

"December. Matt's party. Jacob was there. Jen and Beth were at the party too. We were all smoking up. Drinking. Toasting you, actually."

"That's nice. So?"

"Shut up. I'm trying to remember. Oh fuck." She stopped walking.

"What?" Peter realized he was talking too loudly. "Tell me," he whispered.

"Jacob," Maggie said, "was the one who brought up the houseboat idea."

"I thought you found out about it from friends at school."

"Yeah, I thought I had. But now that I think of it, he was saying that was the best place to party."

"What?"

"Yeah. He said high school and college girls come down here all the time, so they can be away from their parents, take their boyfriends, meet up with guys, et cetera…"

"And you were going to meet Jacob down here? Was that the plan?"

"No. Like I said, he's been my hookup. That's it. This is weird. This is too weird. I don't understand."

"Well, there's nothing to understand. The guy's a freaking hippie douchebag who's dealing weed to score with high school virgins."

"I'm not in high school anymore," Maggie interrupted, "and I'm not a virgin either."

"Let me finish. Douchebag hippie who's wandering around a subterranean tunnel that goes from the middle of an island, under the river somehow, and ends up back at the marina where we rented the houseboat in the first place. This ponytail-wearing motherfucker is leading a group of old men, one of whom looks like my granddad, by the way—"

"Which one?"

"Bill—Mr. Call the CB If You Need Help, Got My Toe Blown Off in the War. He looks like my dad's dad. Anyway, so this ponytail prick is marching up and down these tunnels. And he just so happens to find us, after we had just escaped from some more goddamn hippies. Murderous ones no less. And now you tell me that maybe—there is a slight chance—that this guy gave you the idea to come down here in the first place? Is that pretty much what's going on here?"

"Maybe," she exhaled. "That marina would only rent to us for this weekend specifically. Remember, we were going to try for the Fourth of July?"

"Yeah, I do. So?"

"So this is that summer solstice weekend—the one where they dance around naked and worship all that ancient pagan shit."

"Who are they?"

"Jacob and his friends."

"The Jacob that you buy weed from," Scott whispered. "The Jacob that told you to come down here. The Jacob that's out running a subterranean posse along with the guy from the marina."

"Yes, that one."

"The one who would only rent you the boat on this specific weekend."

"Yes."

"So if I have this correctly—just to make sure...," Peter said. "You are telling me that that Jacob and his friends—the guys that just kicked the crap out of me and tied us up—are not in fact actually dirty peace-loving hippies, but rather probably more like a bunch Satan-worshiping, ritualistic murdering fucks. Fuck!"

"Yeah," Maggie said wide-eyed and distantly. "I wonder where Jen and Beth are."

"Fuck. You're right," Peter slowed down. "Sorry."

"Don't worry about it." She squeezed his arm. "I don't know what the fuck is going on either. We just need to keep calm and make it through the night."

"I should be the one saying that," Peter said.

"We'll get through this together," she said. They both slowed their pace and walked for a few moments in silence.

"Did you hear what they were chanting back there?" Maggie said.

"Yeah. Same as your buddy Pinky. Axel Rose or something." Peter said.

"Axulche. Ever heard of that?"

"Nope."

"I need a fucking cigarette," she said as she plopped down under a tree. They were under a canopy of broad leaves.

Peter sat and faced her. "I'm exhausted. Can we rest for a minute?"

She lay out on the ground. He rubbed her bare arms. She cried. He lay next to her and pulled her bruised body close with his battered arms.

"We're going to be okay," he whispered. "You're right. We're together. We'll make it. I'm right here."

"But you left me," she said.

His heart broke.

"But I came back," he said. He listened to his heartbeat.

"Promise you won't ever again?" she said at last before falling asleep.

"Promise," he whispered, fighting to stay awake. Sleep soon overtook him, and the two lay defenseless in the grass and mud of the island floor.

32

Jerrod turned from Mandy's severed head and threw up in disgust. Beth ran up behind him, saw the atrocity, and started screaming. Jerrod wiped his mouth, came back to upon hearing Beth's screams, and started looking around. He couldn't see or hear anyone. He held Beth and tried to calm her.

"We need to get some weapons," he said. "We need to go back in there and get some knives, or whatever we can find."

"I'm not going back in there with those dead bodies. What could have done that?"

"I don't know, but I think they are out here now." His heart was pounding. "If we don't get something to defend ourselves with, we're next. Plus, I need some clothes."

"Go get them and come back," she said, her head in his chest.

"Are you kidding me?" He pulled back to look at her. "Split up? No. Come on. I'll go first, and you stay behind me."

She nodded silently and brushed tears off her cheek with her palm. Jerrod held her hand, and the two crept back to the boat wreck. Jerrod climbed up first and then pulled Beth up. They tiptoed as quietly as possible into the cabin, stopping every few steps to listen: nothing but frogs and crickets in the night.

Jerrod gathered his Red Hot Chili Peppers t-shirt and pulled on his swim trunks. Beth zipped up her raincoat over her tank top and shorts and put on her gray Vasque hiking boots. They avoided the other bedrooms. The noxious smell was an unmistakable warning to avoid the horror inside. Jerrod found a pack of smokes out on the table, lit one up, and then searched the kitchen for weapons. He found a handful of butter knives but left those on the counter when he found two large butcher knives. He held on to one and put the other on the table for Beth.

Knife in hand, he cautiously walked back past the bedrooms and out onto the mangled stern. He held his breath and looked out over the water: nothing but the moon, the frogs, bugs, and him. The clouds were gone. The rain was gone. The water was still. He took a drag, exhaled, and then left the smoke in his mouth. He avoided the torn fiberglass jutting out below his feet and looked around for the fishing gear. After a minute he found it hidden under the bench that was now forced up through a broken window. He pulled it free, opened it, and pulled out a long thin fishing knife and a plastic box of barbed hooks. Back inside, Beth had picked up the kitchen knife and was also holding a can of pepper spray.

"I've never had to use this," she said. "My dad gave it to me when I started OCC last year."

"If anything comes within ten feet of us, you spray the shit out of them."

"Jerrod…," Beth said.

"Yeah?" he paused.

"Is my sister dead?"

"No. We are going to find Jen, and we are going to slaughter whoever took her."

"Do you think Maggie is dead?"

"No, Maggie's not dead. Scott's not dead. Peter's not dead."

"But these people are dead." She pointed with her knife at the bedrooms. "What makes you so sure we aren't going to die?"

"Because we are going to live forever. That's why."

"But how do you know they won't slaughter us?" she asked, staring at her knifepoint.

He mashed his cigarette out on the table. "Because you were the fastest runner in school, and they aren't going to catch you." He walked up to her and stole a kiss. "And because you're going to spray the shit out of anything that gets near you, and then you're going to stab them to death once they're blinded." He took a deep breath. "And because we're the baddest mother-fuckers on this godforsaken island."

"Anyone who touches my sister is dead," she said, and smiled.

"Fuck yeah."

Beth picked up can of Old Style off the floor, cracked it open, and slammed half the beer. She threw what was left through a window, sending shards of glass and beer into the night. "Anyone who even looks at my sister is dead."

"Fuck yeah."

"We're going to kill a lot of people tonight, aren't we, baby?"

"Fucking-a double-fuck," he growled, slamming his own beer and throwing the empty can at the sink. He shook his fishing knife in the air. "Let's rock."

For a moment, the two locked wild eyes, hyperventilating in terror. Then they sprinted out over the stern, landed on their feet, and ran like knife-wielding lunatics into the heart of the island.

33

They followed the trail through the thick trees and brush, racing each other. Beth was the fastest girl—fastest student—at DHS. Once, a boy had bet ten dollars he could beat her. She crushed him. She kept running after high school, running the track almost every morning before classes at Ogle County College. Now she ran like a cheetah, a knife in one hand and the pepper spray in the other. Jerrod raced to keep up, his heart pounding and breathing short. Adrenaline surged through both, fueled by fear, anger, and revenge. They ran through a tight spot in the trail where the trees seemed to close in on them. Thorny, snarled branches reached in at them, ripping their arms, snapping into their faces. They slowed to a walk as they fought their way through.

Beth wondered if the trail was coming to an end. Did we go the wrong way? What way are we even going? Is Jen alive?

Jerrod held the fishing knife in his mouth and pushed back the thick brush so the two could squeeze through. They saw a light up ahead. The branches cleared. They ran up toward the light, then Beth paused and Jerrod stopped. It was a small wooden cabin, with a light coming from inside, and movement. People were in there. Jerrod and Beth veered off the trail into the brush.

"How do you want to do this?" Jerrod whispered.

"You think we should ask for help?"

"I don't know. Whoever is in that dump could be the killers."

"Yeah, thinking the same thing."

"Okay, let's sneak up and try to get a look at them." Jerrod took a deep breath. "If you see Jen, don't make a sound. Let's see how many there are. You ready for this?"

"Ready."

"Go."

They snuck up from between the trees, trying to not make so much as a twig snap under their feet. The front of the cabin had a wide porch with a hole for a window, and the door was wide open. They circled around the cabin until they found that the far side had another window. This one was partially covered with tattered leather. They heard laughing and froze. After a few more seconds, they heard laughing again from inside the cabin. No one seemed to be outside. They crept up silently, weapons in hand, approached the window, and then Jerrod peered in, trying to breath as quietly as possible. Beth could hear her heart pumping blood through her veins.

Two young men with long dreadlocks were sitting in wooden chairs across from an older man with a long white beard. They were looking down at something. Jerrod strained to see. A little kid was standing in the middle of the room, lighting something on fire. What the fuck? No wait. It wasn't a kid. What Jerrod saw made him gasp. Standing in the middle of the filthy room was a beady-eyed midget, covered with long mossy strands of gray hair. His face looked like a deformed rat, with a long nose, little shiny black eyes, and an extreme overbite.

Jerrod crouched down instantly. He covered his lips with his knife blade and then held up four fingers. Beth nodded. Then he tried to make three and a half fingers. She looked puzzled, so he waved that away and went back to four.

"Four?" she mouthed silently.

He nodded his head. He pointed at her and then at himself, and then toward the front door. She nodded. With extreme caution they tiptoed around the cabin toward the front. As they did, they heard something up ahead. Someone was coming up the trail. They froze and waited, barely visible, or so Beth hoped. Two forms materialized from the trail: one short and one taller. Beth thought it looked like her sister. She started to walk out, but Jerrod stopped her by grabbing her wrist and yanking her down. It wasn't Jen. It was the girl they had seen on the fishing boat the day before, and she was with the man Jerrod had thrown the log at.

The man was dragging the girl. She didn't seem happy to be there. She had a frightened look on her young face. The man pulled her up in front of the steps of the cabin. Jerrod heard a shuffling inside and then saw the backs of the two longhaired men as they sauntered out to meet the man and girl.

"This is Maria—just like I told you," Jesus Reyes said.

"She looks young," Ben said.

"She just turned twelve," Jesus said.

"All right. You can leave her with us," Abe said, walking down the steps.

"No," Jesus stood in front of her. "The deal was, I come with."

"That's not how it works," Abe said, walking up to him. Abe stood a few inches taller. "First we take her, and then you meet Mom."

"No. Tonight's the night. You know that. I know that. Take me with, or she comes back with me."

"Boys," the old man said from on top of the porch, "invite them in. Where are your manners? Mr. Reyes, is it? We are honored that you are able to join us tonight. And just look at how beautiful young Maria is." He held out his long, scab-covered arm. "Come to me, girl. Let's get a look at you."

34

Beth wanted to see in, so Jerrod crouched out of the way. Beth stared into the cabin through the tiny slit in the leather window. The two dreadlocked boys and the old man sat back down at the table. The midget thing disgusted Beth, and she almost made a noise when she saw him. He waddled up to Maria and started poking and prodding her, mumbling to himself. Jesus looked down without any expression.

"How's she looking, Max?" Ben asked.

Max didn't respond but kept examining her, stroking his scraggly chin with one greasy hand. "Hmm, hmm," he whined.

Maria didn't seem fazed at all. She stood in the middle of the room, taking the smelly midget's inspection as if she didn't notice a thing. She wore a white cotton dress that accentuated her light caramel skin and raven-black hair. The midget spun her around and sniffed her bottom like he was a dog.

"Hmmm, hmm…yes, yes." He looked her over once more."Okay, she'll do," he finally said, in a surprisingly deep voice. "You've traveled far to be here, Mr. Reyes."

"I hope tonight is worth the trip," Mr. Reyes responded, with a grin.

Max giggled, waddling back over to a chair next to the other three, and pulled himself up. The floor was littered with a heap of bones of all shapes and sizes. Beth was so mesmerized by the people inside that it startled her when she realized how filthy the cabin was inside. Bones? Really? There is no doubt this is bad, she thought. Jerrod tugged at her raincoat, but she batted him away and kept watching.

"Come join us," Max said. "I've got something to get us in the mood." He pulled out a joint, struck a match on his pants, then lit the joint and inhaled deeply. He held his breath and then offered up the burning joint to Jesus, who was still standing next to his daughter. Jesus hesitated and then pulled up a chair, leaving Maria standing on her own. He took a deep drag and passed to the old man.

Beth saw the tattoos covering Jesus's forearms. She saw the scythe and the black cowl of Death.

The old man inhaled in turn and passed the joint on to Ben. The brothers both smoked the same way—reverently, and in touch with every nerve of their body as the smoke filled their lungs. Abe got up and handed the joint back to Max.

"Maxamilian," Jesus said, "do you really think it's going to happen?"

"Of course"—he inhaled, held his breath, and then exhaled—"it will. You have doubt?"

"None whatsoever," Jesus replied. "What is it like?"

"Rapture. Eternal light. Warmth. Life. Death. How can I possibly describe it?"

"Axulche," Ben said, pondering the gravity of the name.

"Axulche," his old man said. "Your mother has spent so long preparing for this very night."

"Axulche," Jesus lipped.

Maria was silent. Beth was transfixed on the group. For a brief moment, she thought the boys' dreadlocks were writhing on top of their heads. She blinked, and the movement was gone. The men all looked high now, sitting back and staring up at the ceiling. Their eyes were bloodshot. Actually, they looked really red, almost like they were glowing. By the time the joint got back around to Abe, it was barely an ember. So Abe took the last toke and flicked it toward the window. His eyes locked with Beth's.

35

"Ay!" Abe yelled. "Someone's watching us, man!" The room exploded as all four men jumped up out of their chairs. Max stood up on his chair. Maria didn't flinch, still staring out into space. Beth was already ten yards into the trees by the time Jerrod pulled himself up. Ben and Abe tore out the front door, leaped over the porch stairs, and landed running. They veered off in opposite directions at full speed, meeting again at the back of the cabin. They both turned toward the side where they had been watched and stood still for a moment. Their eyes blazed red in the night, and their dreadlocks were, in fact, whipping wildly overhead. Ben could hear Jerrod fleeing, Abe could smell Beth's sex as she ran. They took off after them, howling and snarling like demons as they caught up to their prey.

Beth ran, with Jerrod close behind, and they could hear the terrible howls behind them. They were closing in. Jerrod's head was insane with fear. Beth picked up speed. Jerrod thought of Beth. He thought of his mom. Then he stopped in his tracks. He turned around. He held the thin fishing knife up in his left hand and the butcher knife pointed down with his right.

"Jerrod!" Beth yelled.

"Get the fuck out of here," Jerrod yelled back. "Get the fuck out of here, Beth," he muttered. He was hyperventilating. His heart pounded away in his chest. The knives rattled in his hands as he trembled to face his death. He took another breath. Then another. Then another. Then he listened. Nothing. A frog croaked. Where the fuck are they? He waited. Still nothing. He took a step back. Then another. Then he turned and jogged. Then he sped up and ran as fast as he could.

Inside the cabin, Max and the old man were shuffling Jesus and Maria toward the back.

"This way, this way," Max panted. "Maria, watch your step. Mr. Reyes, please watch your head," he said, as he opened a small door that led to a winding staircase. Jesus paused, looking quizzically at Max and then the old man. "No time, no time. Don't worry about them, they'll take care of whatever's out there—I can assure you."

"When do we meet Hosanna?" Jesus said.

"Soon, very soon," the old man said. "She can't wait to meet you."

"Mother can't wait to see us all," Max said. "But we must go now." He pulled Maria by her hand down the stairs.

Maria followed without emotion. Jesus followed her closely, with the old man bringing up the rear.

Jesus noticed the machete the old man had picked up. He also noticed the light flickering far below that lit their steps as they walked down. The stairs wound so far down that the end was out of site. Max hurried them along, and whenever Jesus stopped to look at the strange markings on the walls, the old, thin man slightly nudged him, walking right up on his back.

Just keep that up asshole, Jesus thought to himself. Another hundred steps down, the air was thick with smoke, with a strange smell. He thought it was like the pot they had all just smoked, but somehow different.

Suddenly, Maria's hair flipped back and forth across her neck, and she started twitching.

"Shh." Jesus put his hand on her shoulder. "It's me—Daddy," he said. "You're fine, just keep going." She started to whimper and squeezed his fingers. "Shh…good girl." Max looked back up with his devilish beady eyes, his forehead covered with sweat. It was hot down here, wherever here was.

"Everything okay back there, miss?" Max asked.

"She's fine," Jesus said. "Just tired. Do you have any water?"

"We have refreshments and snacks waiting for everyone. We're almost there."

As they curved around another time, Jesus saw the floor approach through the smoke. They stepped onto the stone floor, and Max led them into a room with torches burning—one on each wall facing the stairs, three total. The torches looked like bundles of dried reeds, and the flame had an eerie green-and-orange glow. The smell was pungent. Jesus's eyes watered, and Maria quietly coughed.

The room had nine wooden doors, three in each wall facing the stairs. Each door had an ancient iron lock with an ornate keyhole.

Max pulled a large key on a piece of twine out from under his shirt, reached up, and inserted the key in the hole of the door second from the left. "Can you give me a hand?" Max offered to Maria.

She looked back at her father, who nodded. She slowly walked up, looking cautiously at Max, then grasped the key with both hands, and turned. It didn't budge. She tried to push harder, but still nothing. Finally, she took a deep breath, shook out her hands, and then put all of her weight into it. The key turned with a groan, and the door unlocked and swung open.

"Good, friend," said Max. "Please say good-bye, for now, to Joseph, our most gracious escort."

"You're not coming with?" Jesus asked.

"I'll wait back here for my boys," Joseph said. "I'll be along soon enough." He was so thin his ribs all protruded through his skin.

"Those boys of yours are quite something," Max chuckled. "Good kids."

"Yessir," Joseph said. "But not too good. Kind of like their old man. Tell Mother I'll be along shortly."

"Sure enough," Max chuckled. Now come on, you two, we're going home." He led the way into the small corridor.

Maria could walk standing up, but Jesus had to bend down. After they were a good distance down the tunnel, Joseph shut the door and pulled out the key. He stepped back to the middle of the staircase and looked up to make sure no one was coming down yet.

He faced the three walls of nine wooden doors. He counted the doors, left to right and back, until he got to thirteen. He stuck the key into the thirteenth door. After that he sat on the staircase, with the machete on his lap.

36

Ben and Abe were facing Jacob and Bill in a clearing. The two brothers still looked demonic with red eyes and hair flailing, despite there being no wind. But they cowered in front of Jacob.

"We just about had two of them," Abe grunted.

"Yeah, we had two of them too, but…" Jacob trailed off, peering at the two.

"We got to get this under control, boys," Bill said. "Or your mother ain't going to be too happy with any of us."

"No problem, dude," Ben giggled. "We've got this island covered."

"The virgin is safely down, right?" Jacob asked.

"Of course, man. As if you have to ask, bro."

"And the others?"

"No, man—no way."

"What about the Mexican?"

"He's cool, man. He went with Max and Dad."

"What?" Jacob said. "I told you not to let him live."

"Just relax," Abe said. "He's down, man. He smoked up with us and everything, you know. And he had his daughter with him. He earned the trip."

Abe and Ben laughed triumphantly and bumped fists.

"That's not good. I told you that guy needed to get taken care of."

"Max thinks he's all right."

"Oh, is Max the boss now? No. Max is a freak. Since when do you start taking orders from him? Especially tonight! Jesus Christ." Jacob rubbed his head. "Okay, here's the deal. We've got at least four or five meat sacks running around this island still, and they cannot—I repeat—cannot be allowed to leave this island."

"Two of them seen me and Tim. And the girl knows Jacob," Bill said.

"Well no shit, Bill," Jacob said. "You mean the girl I convinced to come down here in the first place? The one that brought all her friends? For the weekend? That one?"

"Yeah, that one. Just saying. And they killed Davis."

"Bummer dude," Abe said.

"And they've seen the tunnel back to the mainland. And they've seen all our neighbors in their holy underwear, and a bunch of other shit they don't need to be telling everyone about. And now, we're getting mighty close to sunrise, fellas." Jacob paused. "You guys high enough to get the job done?"

"Yeah," Ben and Abe both said.

"Need anymore—just to top off?" Jacob asked. They shrugged and nodded their heads.

"Okay, because I just happen to have something for both of you." Jacob busted out two thin joints held in a fist. He offered one to each of his two younger brothers. "Now light those up, puff away, and then do your job. Bill and I are going to lead the rest of the folks down, and you join us when you're done."

"Oh, thanks, broseph," Abe said, already lighting up. "Man, I'm getting the munchies."

Jacob and Bill walked swiftly away in the direction of the houseboat. The two brothers stood in the clearing and smoked, the full ripe moon shone directly overhead. As they smoked, their hair shook and came to life, their eyes grew deep red again, their eyebrows and beards grew and tangled, their fingers tightened and curled, their mouths contorted. Their teeth gnashed, their muscles rippled under their skin, their wounds opened and festered, scabs tore and popped, their joints tightened, and they screamed and howled as the smoke transformed them into bloodthirsty monsters. They set out on the hunt once again.

37

Bill and Jacob found their neighbors calmly sitting inside the houseboat. They announced they were ready. The women stood up first, and each untied the knot that held their toga up on their body. The white clothes dropped to the floor. Each stood naked on the boat. Aged, wrinkled, sagging breasts flopped down on their stomachs. Each woman had long white hair. Tall, thin, fat, short, and all naked. The cop was already naked and stood up from the table. The remaining men removed their clothes, leaving them where they fell. Bill took off his shirt, dropped trou, and jumped in line.

Jacob stayed clothed. He took a head count of the old and naked lineup—thirteen in all. "Hosanna is expecting you," he said warmly.

"Praise be to Hosanna," they replied.

"Axulche is expecting you," he said grandly.

"Praise be to Axulche," they chanted.

"Tonight is the last night we die," he said with conviction.

"Tonight is the last night in one thousand years," they sang.

"One thousand years of godliness," he said.

"One thousand years of God," they said.

Jacob spun on his heels and led the procession back off the boat. He had walked these steps up the beach so many times, tread this island trail so many days and nights. So many rehearsals. So many practices. So many sacrifices. And now here we are, he thought. Wow. What a mindfuck. He walked now, without looking back, keeping a keen eye on the path in front of him, looking and listening for signs of Maggie and her pathetic friends. Probably not long for this world, he thought. Too bad—she was a good lay. Stupid though. Easily persuaded. He remembered lying in bed with her, smoking a pipe. The same shit his brothers had been smoking for years. Why did they get like that? Why didn't he? Why didn't she? Mother's little secret, he guessed. He was glad he didn't. He was comfortable in his role. He got to leave the island. He got to recruit. He always was a good recruiter. "Quick-witted," his mom always said. Sharp. Good judge of character. Ben and Abe are so much more powerful. But it's animal power, not real power. This is right. This is good. Help these good folks. Take care of the family. Yeah, Maggie served her purpose all right. His most important assignment. The biggest event of his life, and he delivered. Thanks to Maggie for bringing Jen along. Who knew there were any teenage virgins left in Dixon?

The barefoot troop followed in single file behind Jacob. Not one mosquito bit their naked flesh. Not one gnat landed on their shoulders. The flying bugs stayed away, as did the crickets, the birds, the toads and frogs. All of nature cleared a wide berth for the thirteen seniors, whose strange pale nudity almost reflected the moonlight. They walked along the ancient trail, humming. Meditating.

"Axulche, soet, cuthsmx, Axulche." Their tongues vibrated in their toothless mouths.

The rocks cut their tender feet, but no one paid notice. They couldn't feel pain. They didn't notice dirt or rocks or the moon or the trees or this earth. They were only aware of Axulche and blessed Hosanna. And they were so hungry. Hungry for the light. Hungry for God. They marched until they arrived at the cabin. Single file, they walked up the front steps, through the filthy kitchen littered with human bones, shuffled through to the small door, crept down, and one by one they descended the ancient winding stairs. These steps brought up gold, thought Jacob. These steps brought up silver and gold and wisdom. He read the ancient carvings all around him on the walls as he led the group down and down. He remembered the stories his mother used to tell him, and now he saw those stories play out over the millennia on the walls—the stories that were his family history, his family tree. The ancient battles. The horrible struggles. The drought, the wars, the famine. The magnificent spectacle his ancestors built on this very ground. The unprecedented monolith that reached to heaven. The deluge of crimson blood that poured down the ziggurat. Blood of the enemy. Blood of the insane that lived in the caves, that saw the first stars. Blood of the children. Our God heard our prayers, he thought. Our God cried for us, not them. His one tear created the lake, and the lake overflowed and surrounded and fed and protected us and our children. He descended the staircase and knew this, and meditated on this, just as everyone else in the line did. They brushed their written history on the walls with their fingertips as they walked by. They knew because they were born knowing, and tonight the river would flow again. Blood and water. Life and death. Axulche.

Jacob met his father at the bottom of the stairs. Joseph opened the door, and the two waited together until the entire party had passed into the tunnel.

"How many are here?" Jacob asked.

"Hundreds."

"Where's the Mexican?"

"I'm going to take care of him right now. Will you stand here until your brothers get back?"

"Of course."

"Take this." He handed him the rusty machete. "I love you, Son."

"Love you, Dad. See you soon."

38

Beth tripped over a log and went hurtling face-first into a tree.

"Fuck," she groaned. The log sat up. It was Peter.

"Peter?" Beth gasped. Someone else sat up. It was Maggie.

"Beth?" Peter said. "Beth! Holy shit! Are you okay?"

Beth dove into Maggie's arms, and they both cried. "Oh my God, I thought I'd never see you again!" she sobbed. "Maggie."

"Where's Jen?" Maggie pulled back.

"Where's Jerrod?" Peter asked.

"Right here." Jerrod ran up panting. "Where's Scott?"

"Scott's dead," Peter said, suppressing tears.

"Jen's missing. We came out here to find her," Jerrod said. "Holy shit, man! You know those older folks, Mandy and her friend. They're dead! Beth and I were literally fucking..." He looked at Beth for a second. "Beth and I were with them on the boat after you guys left. Their boat hit ours, and then they were slaughtered."

"Their boat hit ours? You're not making sense," Peter said.

"None of this makes sense. It's fucking crazy," Jerrod said. "Can we all agree that this is the worst fucking vacation we've ever gone on? And when we do get out of here, and we all want to go somewhere, like spring break or something, we agree we aren't going anywhere near a fucking river?"

"How about we all get out of here and move out of the fucking country," Beth said. "Canada doesn't let this shit fly."

"Here's the fucked up part. There's this cabin—" Jerrod started.

"That's where they killed Scott!" Maggie stood up, her crying stopped. "Some old guy with a nasty beard swung an ax right through his fucking neck. And then these two crazy hippies grabbed me and were saying they were going to eat me."

"Yeah, we saw them. They were smoking some fucking dope with a rat-looking midget. And then that fucking beaner from yesterday showed up. You know—the guy covered in tats who kung fu'd my ass. And he was, like, giving up his daughter in exchange for smoke."

"This is so fucked up. Those crazy hippie assholes were chasing us not twenty minutes ago. We kept running. How fucking big is this island? We've been running forever."

"I can't believe Scotty's dead," Jerrod said. "Number seven. Johnny fucking quarterback. Dead at nineteen."

"Jen's dead," Beth said. "I know it."

"No, you don't know it," Maggie said. "They didn't kill the girl that was with the Mexican guy. Maybe they didn't kill her. You said that they slaughtered those people from the other boat?"

"Yeah."

"And Jen was missing after that?"

"Yeah."

"Well, maybe they took her somewhere. Peter and I fell down a well somewhere around here, and ended up walking out of some fucked up underground river into that creep from the marina…" She trailed off, thinking about Jacob. Fuck it, might as well come clean.

"You guys remember when I suggested that we come down here and rent this houseboat?"

"This was your idea?" Jerrod asked.

"Listen, Jerrod, this could be important," Maggie said. "I knew one of the guys we ran into in the tunnel."

"Yeah, great guy. Her drug dealer."

"Your drug dealer is on this island?"

"No, his name is Jacob. And he fucking tied us up and took us back to this crazy cult that was waiting for us back at the marina."

"Wait…Jacob? Not that Jacob," Beth said.

"Yes, that Jacob."

"Maggie, why are we here?"

"I don't fucking know. I swear. It sounded like a good idea—the boat, the river, the friends. I didn't know he would be here."

"It doesn't matter. Maggie, do you have any feelings for this guy?" Peter asked.

"Fuck no."

"And Jen could still be alive. So the four of us need to agree on something real quick."

"I'm listening," Jerrod said.

"Everyone in town is in on this shit—the marina guy, the fucking cop, a bunch of naked grannies. We've seen it all. I think this whole fucking town parties crazy-style. So there's no point in thinking we're getting any help." Peter paused for a response, but didn't get any, so he continued, "We've got two crazy-ass mofos tearing ass through this forest looking for us. Assuming they live here, it's probably a safe bet that they know this island a hell of a lot better than we do, and will probably find us at any moment. When they do, they will try to kill us."

"Probably," Maggie said.

"Sohoho, my good friends, I think we each need to find at least two weapons."

"Got 'em." Jerrod held up his knives.

"The three of us each need to find two weapons."

"Got 'em." Beth held up her pepper spray and knife.

"Maggie and I both need some weapons," Peter said. "We head back to that cabin. Find Jen. Kill anything else that moves."

"Let's do it," Jerrod said. "Here." He handed Peter the fishing knife. "This should tide you over for now."

Beth gave Maggie her spray and kept her knife.

"Balls to the wall, let's kill 'em all."

"Every time you lose your mind," Maggie said, "every time you want to collapse in terror, every time you want to quit, you remember that they butchered Scott Hey—your friend and mine—and you make them fucking pay!"

Peter surged with confidence as they ran. The four were like ancient warriors. Sharp weapons in hand, fit, in the prime of their physical lives, and they were on the warpath. The sun would be up in just a few more hours. Would they be alive to see it? He didn't care. I'm going to live forever. We will live forever. Why would this not be so? We've made it this far. We're unstoppable.

"No, no, no, no, you can't fuck," he sang as the pack ran.

"Can't fuck with the Ducks!" Jerrod finished.

"Go Ducks!" Beth shouted.

"Go D-town Ducks!" Maggie called out her cheer.

They ran down the middle of the tight path, through the trees, and burst out into the opening in front of the cabin. The demon brothers collided with them, hair writhing and teeth bared with an inhuman fury.

Ben knocked Beth to the ground and immediately set on tearing her apart. Peter stabbed him in the neck with the knife and broke off the handle. Jerrod swung viciously back and forth at Abe. Maggie kicked Ben off Beth and then sprayed him in the face. Ben screamed and clawed at his eyes, and Beth picked up the knife and stabbed him in the stomach. Abe overcame Jerrod and tried to bite him in the face. Jerrod dodged the attack, and Abe took a bite out of his shoulder. Jerrod howled in pain and scrambled to get free. Abe's dreadlocks attacked and whipped him in the face as he clawed and bit and punched and kicked.

Beth slid her knife out of the deep wound she had just given Ben, held it up in the air, and froze for a brief second. The moonlight shimmered on the thin, sharp steel blade. Then she swung down hard, driving the knife all the way up to the hilt into Ben's crotch. She didn't know if she hit scrotum, penis, or thigh. All she knew was that she got something, because Ben screamed like nothing she'd ever heard and started scrambling to get away. She pulled the knife out again and kept stabbing. Abe stopped attacking momentarily to see what was happening to his brother, giving Jerrod the chance to jerk free and knee him hard in the chin. Abe attacked with renewed fervor, gauging and lunging in for the call.

"Yo, freakshow," Peter said. Two red glowing eyes were aimed hot up in his direction. "Smoke this," he added, and cracked a thick branch across Abe's face. Abe's head cranked to the side, and he slumped over.

Jerrod got up. He spit on Abe and then kicked him. Maggie and Beth were kicking Ben repeatedly in the ribs and face.

The two brothers were dragging themselves away, slower and slower, through the blood pouring out of their mouths and wounds. The buzz was wearing off as searing pain was setting in. They wanted Mother. They wanted Dad and Mom. They wanted Jacob to come. They wanted dinner, but dinner was fighting back. Dinner was going to kill them. Ben threw up in terror at the realization that he was dead. He didn't want to die, he wanted to see his mother in light.

"We'll take you to them," Ben said. "Don't kill us. We'll take you to your friend."

"She's alive?" Beth shouted at him, and kicked him again. "Where is she? Tell us now!"

"You'll never find her unless we take you there." Ben waited for a sign—any sign that they would believe him, give him some time.

"Yes, we will. We know she's somewhere in your shithouse over there," Jerrod said.

"No. You'll never get to her in time. We can get her for you."

"Do you have names?"

"Yeah, these shitheads have names," Peter said. "Ben and Abe. Don't know which one's which."

"I'm Ben," Ben said. "He's Abe, my baby bro." Abe wasn't moving.

"You two have killed a lot of people, right?" Peter asked.

Ben nodded his head.

"How many of you are there?"

"Just us."

"Okay. So there are four of us and two of you."

Ben shook his head again.

"Jerrod, can I see that knife of yours for a second?" Peter asked.

"Sure thing," Jerrod said. He flipped the large knife over and handed it to Peter handle-first.

"You want to live, don't you, Ben?"

"Yeah."

"And you're going to show us where our friend is?"

"Yeah, I promise."

"You're fucking right, you promise," Peter said. He glared at Ben as he walked over to Abe. He picked up Abe's head by the dreadlocks, pulled him to the side so his face was pointed directly at Ben's, and then violently slit his throat from ear to ear. He carved the butcher knife as deep as he could through the skin and muscles and tendons and dug it deep into the spine. Blood exploded onto Ben's face—his brother's blood. "That's for Scott, you evil bastard. Next time it's you, if anything happens to Jen Miller. Do you fucking understand?"

Ben sobbed in terror. He licked his lips, craved the blood, resisted the urge, fought the urge, dreaded the thought, vomited, and then shit himself. And then he lunged for his dear brother's corpse. His attackers jumped back in shock as he feasted on the neck cavity, unable to overcome his addiction for flesh. His world was ruined, and he sobbed and feasted. Neck meat. The sweetest.

39

Maggie watched in detached amazement as Ben gulped from his brother's corpse. He was like a German Shepard on a T-bone.

"Don't go near his mouth," Peter said.

"No shit," Beth answered. "Does he even know we're here anymore?"

"All right," Maggie said, "time to go. We need to find Jen, remember?"

Ben kept eating. Jerrod kicked him off the dead body. Ben's face was covered in blood and gore. He looked around, disoriented, and then fixed his stare on his brother.

"Take us to our friend. Now," Peter said.

"All right," Ben said, with a new calm. His eyes weren't glowing anymore. His hair didn't move.

He looked like what Maggie remembered of him before—just a hillbilly, backwoods piece of shit, with blood and scabs all over. Ben pulled himself up, wiped off his mouth, and limped toward the cabin. The four followed.

"Why the fuck," Jerrod said, "did you just drink your own brother's blood?"

"Couldn't help it, man," Ben said. "Blood, you know."

"Do you eat people?"

"I have."

"Why?"

"Why does the dog chase the cat?"

"Instinct," Beth said.

"Instinct," Ben repeated.

They arrived at the cabin. Keeping an eye on Ben, who seemed so different than the monster he was just moments ago, they searched the cabin for signs of others. Peter sat Ben down at the big table then inspected a few of the bones strewn about the floor. Some would be big enough to hit someone with, but he wanted something bigger. Maggie found the ax lying in a corner—the same ax that had been used to split Scott nearly in two, right before her eyes. She handed the bloody ax to Peter. A loud motor noise broke the silence, and they all jumped.

Jerrod emerged from a back room revving an old chainsaw. He waved the blade inches from Ben's face. "Let's go, motherfucker," he shouted. He revved the chainsaw full power.

Ben got to his feet and walked over to the small door in the back. He opened the door slowly, listening to the chainsaw idling.

"Wait," Peter said. He walked in ahead, gazing down the endless chasm between the spiral stairs. "Who's down there waiting for us?"

"No one. Your friend is locked in a room at the bottom of the stairs. I'm telling you, it's just us."

"He's lying," Beth said.

"Of course he's lying. What about your old man? What about all the townies?"

Ben stared at them silently, bloody lips sealed.

Peter tossed something between the stairs. "Guess we'll find out now, won't we?" He ran down the spiral stairs, ax in hand.

Jerrod shoved Ben in front of him, prompting him along with the idled blade of the saw. Ben got the message and started moving. Jerrod and Maggie ran behind him. Beth scooped up a hatchet from the floor and followed.

40

Jacob sat at the bottom of the stairs, machete across his lap, just like his father had done before him. And just like his grandfather had done before him. He was the protector. He kept the food supply coming. And most importantly, he kept his mother happy. Not that it was easy. It was challenging. But it was worth it. Who was he to complain? He was following in the path of the elders. Tonight was a wondrous and terrible moment in the entire history of the universe, and he played a key role…

Something hard and heavy sailed past him at lightning speed, exploding next to him on impact. Bone and blood and skin splattered all over him. He jumped up. A pulp of hair and mess lay at his feet. He stuck it with the tip of his machete and hoisted it up. He swallowed when he recognized the remains of his brother Abe's head. He swung it off his sword in disgust and then looked up the stairs. He heard commotion. He stepped back, took a deep breath, checked his watch, and then steadied himself, holding up his blood-dipped blade.

41

Jesus and Maria followed the waddling midget through a maze of corridors, some that Jesus had to actually crawl through. He led them through twists and turns, switchbacks and blind corners.

"How old are these tunnels?" Jesus asked, noticing the numerous carvings along the walls.

"Before white man," Max said, annoyed to answer his question. "Before you."

"This used to be above ground?"

"Parts of it. For years, this place teemed with people. We lived here, worshiped here, played here, had families. It was beautiful."

"You speak of those days like you were there," Jesus said.

Max didn't respond. They turned another corner, and then the tunnel gave way to a vast cavern. Jesus's torch filled the room with orange light. Maria looked around at the stalagmites and rock formations. Giant purple and white crystals hemorrhaged all around them. Fifty feet up, the cavern ceiling was dripping with water and sediment. Max scurried on a well-worn trail through the middle of the cavern and guided them up over a ledge.

Just when Jesus was getting his mind around the room, he hiked over the ledge and back down a small passageway made by a crack in the rock. Then Jesus heard something. Down the long tunnel, he heard singing. As the tunnel floor smoothed out, Max hurried in front, looking back and waving them on urgently. The chanting grew louder. Now Jesus could see something up ahead. Light, more light, and motion. It seemed like the whole end of the tunnel was moving. He thought it looked like white worms gyrating and singing. Maria stopped walking ahead of him and stood still. He gently nudged her on. Max impatiently ran back to pull her hand.

As they got to the end of the hall, Jesus saw what he had mistakenly thought were worms. They were people. Naked. Hundreds of them. Packed wall to wall. Singing and chanting a language long forgotten. Hands in the air, old arm flab sweating into the massive cavern. He couldn't believe how many people were here. They were all old, covered in dirt, and in a trance. The torches mounted on the cavern walls were burning the same green-orange glow. The air was thick with smoke and the stench of sweat—and fish. Dead fish. The cavern ceiling was so high above them that they almost seemed to be in the open night air.

Above the crowd, Jesus saw slabs of meat dangling from large iron hooks. Chains ran hundreds of feet up to the cavern ceiling. He realized the meat had been human. The mangled corpses hung upside down, hooks lodged in the rib cages and backs. Some were missing heads, some, arms or legs. Black blood dripped onto the gathering below. They weren't just covered in dirt. Their naked bodies were smeared with filth and blood.

He saw a plume of smoke rising from the naked fleshy mass, rising all the way up, hundreds of feet, to a hole in the middle of the ceiling. The smoke billowed straight up through the soaring hole and into the night. Maria looked back at him, and he saw the fear in her eyes. He looked at her without betraying emotion and nodded for her to follow Max.

As Max held Maria's hand and pulled her into the room, the crowd naturally parted to give them passage.

They're not even looking at us, Jesus thought. The old congregation chanted and danced in their places, shoulder to shoulder, but they seemed to be aware of their presence. They parted so that a path formed, and Max, Maria, and Jesus walked into the pit of the crowd. The women and men engulfed them into the crowd, closing the gap slowly as they walked in. They walked under the hanging, yellowed corpse of what had been a young girl. Blood trickled out of the neck cavity, and a drop landed on Jesus's head as he passed under.

He looked down and noticed one of the old women was missing her big toe on her left foot. Then he noticed the man standing next to her was missing his big toe also—same as before, left foot. He quickly surveyed the entire group. All missing the left big toe. Yep, he thought. Right place. He shook off his fear and looked ahead. As if there was any question. He still couldn't see the source of the smoke, but that's where they were headed. As he got closer, he smelled something besides fish. He smelled something besides sweaty old bodies. Whatever it was smelled good.

The last few dancers moved out of the way, and the sheer immensity of the cavern was finally revealed. Opened up in front of them was a massive lake of ink-black water. Jesus's eyes trained across the surface of the water. It appeared to be moving, bubbling. No, something was in the water. The lake stretched hundreds of yards across to the opposite side, where a bonfire was raging, casting the gray-black column of smoke into the night. Jesus's eyes followed the surface of the water. He watched the fire on the far side of the lake. There were people over there, but they were too distant to see in the dim light.

"Come, come," said Max, and took them down to the water's edge.

Jesus definitely saw flashes of motion in the water. Must be teeming with fish. Black rolling shapes appeared and disappeared on the surface. A small wooden boat was coming toward them with a few people inside. He checked behind him. The throng of naked people hadn't moved. They were just swaying in place. Their eyes were either closed or glazed over. They were chanting in a bizarre pattern, dancing, and meditating. As the boat approached, he could see it carried four men across the water. They were clothed in tattered overalls and jeans. Their faces looked peculiar as they approached, unnaturally clenched. They pulled up to shore and stepped onto the rock. Max pulled the boat farther out of the water.

"One more for Mother," Max said. "Isn't she a beauty?" The men approached Maria. "Your trip is almost finished, young lady," Max said, looking up at her with a sincere look of accomplishment. "These good boys will now escort you across. No more tunnels, no more stairs. You can finally rest."

The four men reached out for her.

Jesus stepped in between them. "She can't go on her own. Come on, Maria." He took her hand. "Let's go."

Two of the men sprang at Jesus, pushing him out of the way and driving him to the floor. The two others took hold of Maria, who screamed for the first time the whole night.

"No one goes across unless Hosanna commands it," Max chastised Jesus. "You stay on this side."

"No!" Jesus struggled. "I stay with my daughter. That was the agreement!"

The two brutes pinned him to the ground.

"I didn't make any agreement. I just let you follow me up until now," Max said as he jumped into the boat.

One held the girl, and the other pushed off. Jesus struggled against the two, but they overpowered him completely. They weren't attacking him though, so he calmed down. After a few moments, they stood up. He stood up. The boat was halfway across the lake, rowing toward the fire. They let go of him but stood between him and the water.

"Maria!" Jesus called past the two guarding him. "Maria!"

"Daddy!" she yelled back, her voice drifting above the water.

He burst in between the two and ran as fast as he could toward the water, his eyes never leaving his beloved daughter. I love you baby, he thought. Hang in there. I'm coming for you. We'll both be back home in no time.

Maria watched him from the boat through tear-filled eyes. She had been aware of her surroundings for the last hour, maybe more. She was petrified. She remembered the plan. She remembered the practice. She remembered what she had to do and say. She remembered she had to stay calm. But she couldn't. Daddy would always be right behind me. Daddy would always protect me in the end. And now she watched her father dive into the lake, calling her name. She saw him dive in, and she saw the water explode with fury all around him. She watched the black water swirl, buzz, and come alive. And she saw great jagged fins cut up out of the water and submerge with shocking speed. She saw the naked throng on the shore surge up behind her dad's attackers, and she saw them all dancing more frantically now as the black lake came alive right in the spot where her dad had been. She jumped up to dive in after him, but the man grabbed her by the waist, and Max shook his head no.

"I'm sorry, my dear," said Max, "but you see, no human can swim in this water and make it back out." She stared at him in horror and then stared at the spot where the water still splashed and surged with violent energy. Her captors rowed her away from the frenzy, away from the massive crowd, and away from her father. She bit her lip and turned to see what lay ahead. Behind the fire, something massive lumbered in the shadows.

42

"You die now!" Peter yelled, as he leaped the final ten stairs and collided with Jacob.

Jacob blocked the blow of the ax with his machete and then swung hard at Peter's shoulder. Ben spilled in behind Peter, which caught Jacob off guard. Then someone new came running down the steps with a chainsaw, and Jacob started wishing he wasn't guarding the entrance. Jerrod squeezed the trigger full throttle, and the noise tore through the room. The chainsaw came down on Jacob's machete, knocking it to the ground. Jacob was defenseless. He jumped back, away from the swinging chainsaw.

"Ben, help me!" he pleaded.

Ben stooped down slowly, as if halfheartedly trying to pick up the machete. But Peter kicked it out of the way. Jacob and Ben both backed up against the far wall. The four faced them, weapons in hand.

"Maggie," Jacob said, "I'm so glad to see you're all right. This isn't a safe place for you."

"No shit," Maggie said. "Or for you. Kill him."

"No wait, wait, wait, wait. What do you want? I can help."

"I want my sister back," Beth said.

"Jen? That's who you are upset about?"

"Yes, Jen. Where is she?"

"I know where Jen is. I can take you there. I can take you where she is right now."

"Your brother here is already going to."

Jacob and Ben looked at each other. Jacob saw how different Ben looked, how boyish and timid. He also noticed his blood-covered mouth.

"What happened to our brother?" Jacob asked.

"He tried to kill us, so we killed him first," Peter said. "And your brother here went into a feeding frenzy when he saw the blood."

Jacob watched his brother as he heard the news. Ben's eyes were completely vacant. He was just a shell now. Useless. He hugged his brother. Peter walked up to pull him off, but Jacob spun around and kicked him in the stomach.

The kick knocked the wind out of Peter. He jerked back, and Jacob grabbed the ax out of his hand. Jerrod raced up with the chainsaw roaring, but Jacob took a full swing and knocked the blade away and then punched Jerrod in the face.

Maggie and Beth both ran at Jacob. He swung wildly—fighting to hit, fighting to kill. Beth chopped with the hatchet. Maggie stabbed with the knife. But he held them back.

Peter shook his head and came back to. Ben stood against the wall.

Jacob screamed a war cry and threw the ax straight at Jerrod's head. Jerrod ducked out of the way and came at Jacob, bringing the chainsaw down right on Jacob's forearms. Blood spattered out of his arms. He screamed in shrill terror as the chainsaw pushed deep down into his arms, cutting into muscle and bone. His blood splattered on Ben's face. Ben licked his lips, savoring the blood. His eyes started to glow again. His hair started to wriggle again.

"Fuck this shit," Peter said, picking up the machete. He ran at Ben with the blade pointed out.

"No! Wait, Peter!" Beth yelled.

But it was too late. As Ben's hair shot up and whipped around like it was on fire, and the blood haze consumed him, Peter drove the machete right into his chest, piercing his heart.

"He knows where Jen is!" Beth cried.

Peter kept pushing the blade deeper and tearing back and forth with it, leveraging the weight of the handle to gouge through his core. Ben slumped, and Peter fell on top of him, then rolled over.

Jerrod stood over Jacob, who was sprawled out on the floor, bleeding and quivering. Maggie stood next to him with her knife.

"Where's Jen?" Maggie demanded.

"It doesn't matter."

She spit on him. "Where's Jen?"

"You'll never get to her in time."

"That's what your dead freak brother told us too. But she's alive. I know it."

"Maggie," Peter said.

"What, Peter?"

"Stop asking questions. No more questions."

"But he knows where she is."

"But he's still playing games with you. Here, look." Peter walked over with the ax, kicked one of Jacob's arms out onto the floor, and chopped his hand off with one swing.

Jacob clenched his bloody stump and howled in pain.

"Where is she!" Peter screamed in his face. "Your other one's next!"

"Here…here," Jacob whimpered. He yanked a key from under his shirt with his remaining hand and tossed it on the floor. "Take it. She's past the third door on the left. Go down the hall, no turns. She's in a cell there. Just leave. Leave me."

Beth picked up the key, walked over to the third door from the left, stuck the key in the keyhole, and struggled to pry it open. The door slowly groaned open into a dark low tunnel.

"Can you see anything?" Jerrod asked.

"I can't tell," Beth said. "Should we stay here with him, or all go?"

"No need," Maggie said. "Jacob, you really were a charmer."

Jacob looked up at her and managed a fake smile through the pain.

"I actually had thoughts for you once," she continued. Peter grimaced. "But, turns out, you are a lying, kidnapping, murderous loser, and I'm just not into that anymore."

Jacob raised one eyebrow. Maggie kicked him in the face. Jerrod kicked him in the ribs. Maggie and

Jerrod took turns kicking him up and down his body. Peter lifted up the ax and swung down, crushing his skull. Jerrod brought the chainsaw down on his stomach, and Jacob exploded into a bloody, gory mess as the two took turns bashing away anything resembling humanity.

Jacob's thoughts drifted toward the tunnel as he was released from his mortal coil. He thought of his mother and his father and his thousands of brothers and sisters. He knew that he had served them well, and he knew he would join them all again soon. He was miles away from Illinois by the time his head was cleaved away from his awful mess of a former body.

43

Jesus immediately found out why he should not have jumped into the lake. Every nerve ending in his body burned as the black water seemed to come alive with electricity. He burned like he was in the middle of a fire. Giant dark shapes attacked him from all sides. Wide mouths, with thousands of razor-sharp daggers for teeth, biting him, jabbing him, and pulling him down. The shock was so great he lost awareness of where he was, and his mind flashed far away. He saw his young wife dressed in white flowing robes. He saw Maria being born. He saw Maria on her first birthday, just starting to walk. He saw her at four years old at her mother's funeral. He saw her studying the ancient books. He saw her practicing her blocking, her kicks. He saw her practicing how to hold a sword and how to shoot a gun. He saw the insane eye of the Gardenhead Worm he slaughtered under Giza. He saw his sword sunk into the coarse black hide of the Ciarraighe forest demon. He saw all his battles at once, clashing impossibly against the enemies of his people. He came back to the present and struggled to go up for air. Hundreds of fish, maybe thousands of fish, swarmed him and attacked him, biting and pulling him down. He was drowning, deeper and deeper in the bottomless well. I love you, Maria, he thought. Do your job, he thought. Do what you were born to do. She was his last thought as he was eaten alive by the horrible beasts in the deep. She was his last thought, until he saw a glowing blue light far below him.

44

Maria turned in the boat and faced away from the stillness on the water, where her father had drowned. She faced away from the massive throng of naked zombies on the far side of the lake, faced away from any memory of the living. Now as they rowed her closer, she saw who sat behind the fire. She saw the immense face lapped by the wicked flames. As the boat touched the shoreline, she saw a horrible queen on her throne.

Max stepped off the boat and immediately fell to the ground, bowing in deep reverence. "Mother," he said, still bowing with his face in the ground, "I have brought you this present, in honor of this most joyous of nights." He stood back up.

"Maxamilian," the queen said. "Welcome home, my child. What a thoughtful gift. You are such a good boy. Now come over here and help your old mother."

The queen sat on a throne of bones. The horrible chair was made of human skulls and femurs mixed with aquatic spines. The queen herself was beyond fat. Naked, her stomach rolls poured over her thighs. Her breasts were the size of sandbags, drooping low to her knees. She wore only a necklace made of sharp, jagged bones and teeth. She was eating something. Something cracked between her teeth as she bit down and chomped. A skeletally thin man hunched over her, massaging her fat. He kneaded and prodded and shook her massive fat rolls as she ate.

Max stripped off his filthy clothes in front of Maria. She was shocked to see how obscenely big his penis was, hanging below his stubby fat legs. He scurried over to his mother and found his patch of fat to massage. They worked, moved, pushed, slapped her fat around, and giggled with her as she ate. She was eating some kind of meat on the bone, like game—rabbit, or something.

Maria stepped closer. She saw bones in a pile at the queen's feet. She saw a small bone in the queen's hand, with meat on it. She saw the tiny bones of fingers. She saw tiny skulls in the fire. She saw meat juices dripping from the obese queen's mouth, dribbling down her chin. Everywhere—children's bones, children's bodies. Children's rib cages and jawbones were in the fire—the fire that danced in the evil queen's black eyes as she feasted on the charred flesh of the Bain boy and girl, caught fresh this very night. She chomped and tore and chewed and swallowed their meat, their flesh and their innocence. Maria threw up. The man from the boat grabbed her and shoved her at the feet of the queen.

Max and Joseph kept working diligently. The queen tossed the little boy's arm into the fire, picked clean of all the meat. Then she belched.

"Help me up," she commanded.

Joseph and Max both climbed up into the throne behind her and pushed with all their might to pop her up out of her seat. Her back end was covered with shit. They struggled and finally forced her up. She towered over Maria now, looking down hungrily. "Do you know what tonight is?" she demanded.

"The night of Axulche," Maria answered.

"Axulche," the queen breathed. "Tonight we are blessed. Tonight we are free. Tonight we are joined by God."

"Praise Axulche." Maria repeated the name from memory.

"You play such an important part. Are you ready, my blessed child?" The queen grinned.

"Yes, Mother."

"You are the seventh and most important, my dear."

"Yes."

"Bring me the sixth," the queen addressed the guard directly for the first time.

He marched behind the bonfire, behind the throne, and emerged moments later with another girl. She had dreadlocks. She was covered in dark blood. Her eyes were vacant, like she didn't know she was there. Maria wanted to save her. She wanted to stop this. But she couldn't. Her dad was dead. The plan hadn't worked. She was alone.

"Axulche soet cuthsmx," the queen said, looking up at the smoke that curled into the night sky high above them. "Axulche comes within the hour. One thousand years we have waited for him."

"One thousand years," repeated Joseph, now peering hungrily at the two girls.

"On thousand years my children have waited for him," the queen said, waving her gargantuan arm toward the lake where the hundreds gathered in a naked mass. "One thousand years of life. One thousand years of blood. Eternity wrapped in his dark blankets of ecstasy!" she cackled. The crowd chanted louder now with building excitement. "Bring that one over here," the queen said.

The guard pulled the other girl in front of his queen mother and then undressed her. Joseph handed his mother, his wife, his sister, and his queen, a long dagger with ornate carvings on the handle. He handed it to her reverently.

The queen took the blade, kissed the iron, and muttered the ancient spell. "Rawsa, faru, vons," she whispered, and then swiftly took hold of Jen Miller's wrist and sliced her outstretched palm.

Jen squealed, terrified. They had taken her off the boat, those horrible demons. They had made her eat something, some kind of fish or slug. She could barely remember. She had woken up in this place. Who are all these people? What is this monster in front of me? Oh my God, where's Beth? Where's everyone? What is she doing to me? She tried to run, but Max tripped her, and she fell to the hard ground, naked and crying. Her hand stung where the fat beast had cut her, and the pain brought her back to reality. Her heart exploded with fear.

The queen caught Jen's blood as it dripped off her hand. She held it in her fat fingers and licked the knife clean like she was licking frosting off a beater. She loved this taste best of all.

"Rawsa faru vons Axulche!" she shouted, and threw the blood drops into the bonfire. "Rawsa faru Axulche soet!"

The bonfire contracted, like it was going out, and then shot up in great red and green flames, into the cavern. The cult on the far side of the lake lifted their heads in unison as the flames lit up their naked bodies. They screamed with delight as the flames lit the entire cavern, as if the sun itself were lighting the expanse. The fire dropped back down, and thick black smoke fanned out from the top of the fire and wafted throughout the cavern instead of circling straight up. The smoke poured over the naked mass of worshippers and circled in their nostrils and mouths. They breathed in deeply and danced and pushed against each other. They laughed and cried and whispered their god's name. They pressed flesh against flesh, caressed and fell into one another. And the smoke bathed them inside and out as they reached for each other's arms and legs, locked in a pulsing, sweaty, and wrinkled embrace. Their eyes turned red, their white hair began to search on its own, their loose skin grew tight, their muscles tightened, and their tendons began to snap. They started to rub harder and deeper, and passion rippled through the pit of erections, firm breasts, luscious lips, wet mouths, vaginas, and supple bottoms. And the smoke whipped them into a frenzy, like nothing they had felt in generations.

45

The shark-sized catfish dragged Jesus Kan B'alam K'inich Reyes down into the depths. Their black, wide-set eyes reflected the blue glow radiating from the bottom. Jesus struggled to pull his arms free, and the razor sharp teeth dug through his tattoo-covered skin. He hollered in pain and let out his last breath. Focusing on the light, his mind exploded with primal rage. The dark water gave way to a bruised purple-blue glow as he descended. Something pulsed under the glow—something covered in veins and sinew and scales. Something humming. Noise. The water was hot. The water was hotter now. The water was near boiling. His skin started to bubble. The catfish scurried downward faster and faster. The pressure was crushing his head.

With one last horrible surge of energy, Jesus broke free of his aquatic captors and pulled a broad knife from his boot. The handle melted into his hand and grafted to his bones. He landed on the radiating abomination knife-first and dug into the sick hide with all his dying might. Maria's face was all he saw as his body exploded. Thousands of black catfish swirled in a danse macabre around their god, spinning and consuming the blood mist offered up in the water. The pulsing blue form that made up the entire lake bottom was quivering now. Brown and red bubbles of filth hemorrhaged from the wound that Jesus had made on impact. Black-red spurts burst into the boiling water, freezing and scabbing and ripping again as more puss-filled buckets of blood poured out of the fissure. The entire lakebed was bubbling now, pulsing and wobbling. An underwater volcano of putrescence erupted out of the wound. The nightmare of fish danced wildly in the bloody black water as the lake shook at its foundation. The blue glow burned brighter, and the catfish that got too close boiled from the inside out, exploding around the red blast of filth and over the blue glow that was steadily filling the entire lake.

46

The four stood panting over the mangled bloody corpse on the stone floor. The green-orange flames flickered up the walls and cast satanic shadows up the ceiling. Beth took a step back and then fell to the ground in shock. Maggie's knife dropped with a clank as she ran to console her. Peter jerked the machete out of Ben's corpse, letting the body slump to the ground. He took a wide swing and sent blood spattering off the blade onto the doors.

"So which one"—he caught his breath—"do we try?"

"That one has a key in it," Maggie said, nodding to the middle door. "Try it out."

Peter turned the key, pulled the door open, and peered into the darkness. All he could see was darkness.

"What's it look like?" Jerrod asked.

"Shh," Peter said, "I'm listening."

They all watched him.

Peter didn't hear anything. He took down one of the remaining torches and held it out into the tunnel. It looked like a small corridor proceeded for five or six feet and then dropped off. He crept up to the ledge and looked over. Bottomless. And across the dark chasm was a solid stone wall. He crouched down. Nothing. No stairs, no rocks to hold on to. Just smooth stone all the way down. He heard something then—something from down below. Something that made his skin crawl. A hot belch of air surrounded his face as he heard it again. A hissing. Or a moan. Whatever it was, he was suddenly gripped with fear. He bolted upright and ran back out the door, slamming it behind him. "Not this one," he muttered, locking the door and quickly pulling out the key. "Anyone else want to try?"

"What was in there?" Maggie asked.

Peter didn't respond, but instead tried to fit the key into the next door. The key didn't fit in the doors to the left or right of the middle door. It did fit in the far left door but wouldn't budge. Jerrod took over but couldn't get it to turn over in the far right. He found it did open the door second from the right, and then found that it also opened the door second from the left. Both open doors revealed small dark passages that disappeared into the black.

"Well," Jerrod said to the group, "what now?"

"We should split up," Beth said.

"Split up?" Maggie said. "That's the dumbest thing we could possibly do. We need to stay together."

"We don't have time," Beth said. "They are doing something to Jen. They said so. She needs us. We don't know which tunnel is the right one. We need to split up."

"She's right," Jerrod said. "Two of us go down this one, and two go down the other. We each have a weapon, and there are enough torches for all of us."

"Fuck," said Peter. "Okay. Maggie, you come with me. Beth, you go with Jerrod."

"Which one do you guys want to try?"

"You pick," Peter turned to Maggie.

"That one." Maggie pointed to the right. They all looked at the black mouth of the tunnel.

"So this is it," Beth said.

"No," Jerrod said. "It's nothing. We're going to go get Jen back, and then we are going to meet back here. We all go up together."

"Love you guys," Maggie said.

"Love you," Beth cried.

The two embraced. Beth hugged Peter and kissed him on the cheek.

"You take care of her."

Peter squeezed her back and nodded. Maggie hugged Jerrod, and then Peter and Jerrod hugged.

"Go fuck yourself," Jerrod said.

"You first, dipshit," Peter replied.

The group took one collective breath. Jerrod struck the edge of the chainsaw on the ground. Beth wielded her hatchet in the air. Maggie grasped her knife. Peter and Jerrod pulled down the remaining torches. Armed with steel and fire, the pairs raced through the doorways. As the room at the bottom of the stairs was enveloped in darkness, ancient creatures slithered out from the cracks in the floor to feast on the bloody remains splayed out across the ground.

47

The men grabbed Jen as she struggled to escape and carried her back over in front of the hideous queen. This isn't happening, Jen thought. She remembered the books she had read at the school library about witches and pagan sacrifices. This witch looked nothing like the wiccans she had seen drawings of. Those misunderstood women were celebrating nature and worshiping Mother Earth, not eating children. Not cutting me. Why am I here? Why am I the one instead of my friends? Who's going to rescue me? Then, as she was forced up, inches from the front of the queen's face, she could see her own reflection in those evil ancient eyes. She could smell the putrid breath of death and blood and ancient rot. And she could see her own reflection. And then she knew. She knew why she was there. The queen saw the understanding and grinned horribly.

"Yes," she croaked. Jen lurched away, but the men held her forcefully right up to their mother. "You're a virgin. The sixth virgin, actually." She cackled and farted with delight. Jen trembled, crying hysterically. Maria stood some feet away and watched, frozen in terror. "You're going to serve a glorious purpose." She patted Jen's cheek with her fat, filthy hand. "You're pure, you understand." Her smile turned to a scowl, and she jerked her head around to face the writhing orgy across the lake. "Look!" she wheezed. "These are my offspring. Everyone you see. Living life. Enjoying the ecstasy of flesh and body. Full of ripe lust. You have never tasted their passion. They are beyond their years, all of them. We are blessed by God. And tonight we give thanks. Axulche will hear my prayers tonight. Seven virgins. Seven prayers. We shall be blessed for another millennium!" She lifted her blood-stained hands up into the swirling smoke.

The two men took Jen to an altar made of bones by the edge of the lake. The altar was covered in blood. Gore dripped down its sharp pointed edges protruding in all directions. The men lifted her up and slammed her down on the top of the altar. She screamed in pain as hundreds of knife-point bones dug into her back and legs. Hosanna loomed over her, facing the wild orgy on the other side of the lake. As Jen's blood dripped off the altar into the water, the whole lake came alive again with splashing and fins curling up out of the surface. Jen squirmed, and the men pulled her down hard, causing the bones to go in deeper. She screamed like a goat being eaten alive by a lion.

"Axulche!" Hosanna cried to the hole in the top of the cavern, her arms outstretched. In her left hand, she clenched the ancient blade. The dagger glowed. Her immense naked body glistened with sweat, her breasts were caked with blood. "Rowsa Soet Axulche! Feast so that we may feast! Drink so that we may drink! Live so that we may live to worship you, oh wonderful lover!" Her eyes rolled back into her head. Her tongue flicked in and out of her mouth. Her arms shook. Her breasts trembled.

Waves appeared on the lake. The naked mass was pounding each other, throttling each other. Blood mist surrounded them all. The black smoke whipped through the cavern, into their nostrils and through the queen. She screamed an orgasmic release and then drove the knife down into Jen's naked white chest, directly between her small breasts. The blade sunk up to the hilt. Jen screamed one last time and then choked on blood. Hosanna inhaled the intoxicating scent of her virgin blood but resisted the overwhelming urge to feast. Not just yet. Her eyes reopened, and she looked over at Maria greedily. Soon, she thought. She turned back to the task at hand. She jerked the knife down from the sternum to Jen's navel, gutting her completely. "My children!" She stepped back. None of them were stopping their thrashing now. They were all violently fucking each other. "Praise be to Axulche," she said quietly. She nodded, and the men lifted Jen's dead body up off the altar and tossed it into the lake.

Jen's lifeless body fell deep into the black frenzy. Her blood and organs poured out of her as she fell. Giant, grotesque fish curled around her and escorted her down. They tangled in her entrails, spinning in her intestines. They danced with her, down, down toward their big brother. They gently gripped her arms and neck with their teeth, pulling her down to serve her final glorious purpose.

48

Maggie and Peter raced down the passage. Peter had to duck because the ceiling was so low. He held out the torch to watch for sudden pits. The hallway went straight only for a bit and then opened up into a cavern filled with stalactites and stalagmites. As they navigated through the sharps rocks, their feet began to splash through standing water.

"Wait," Maggie said.

Peter stopped. "What?"

"Listen."

They both stood still. Peter thought he could hear something.

Maggie nodded. "Sounds like voices. That way."

They started walking again. Peter stepped on something squishy and almost twisted his ankle. He jumped back and held down the torch.

"What the fuck!" he said. Squatting in two inches of water was a human face staring back at them. "Jesus Christ, what the fuck is that!"

"Oh gross," Maggie said.

The face looked up at them and then suddenly flipped around in the water and scurried away.

"Oh, sweet fuck!" Peter said. "It's alive!"

The head had a tail and flippers behind it. Peter swung his torch around by the water's surface. Hundreds of eyes stared up at them.

"Oh gross, oh gross, oh gross!" Maggie yelled. "Get the fuck out of here!"

Peter started swinging his machete in the water. He struck one of the fish faces, cutting right through it like a sick bowl of Jell-O. He kicked the next one and sent it flying across the room, splatting against a rock outcropping.

"Come on," he said. "They're harmless."

Maggie did a scoop-kick to get one of the green faces out of her path. The faces just stared at them blankly, never blinking, barely moving. Their fat lips and flabby noses quivered in the shallow water. The two cleared a path through the Jell-O fish faces and kept on toward the voices. They saw a large, dark hole in the opposite side of the cavern, which looked like the way out. Then the hole moved. Peter punted one of the fish faces in its direction. The head made contact with the black mass and bounced off. The dark shape made three bouncing motions and turned around. It was a greenish-gray human face, the size of a truck, staring back at them. The hairs on the back of Maggie's neck stood up. That's the mom, she thought. Then it rushed them.

Peter charged and swung at the monster face with his machete. He lopped off the nose, but the mouth grabbed his entire leg. The face's massive tail and flippers shook violently, causing the head to whip Peter up and down against sharp rocks. Peter beat at it with the machete. Maggie jumped in and stabbed it repeatedly in the eyeball with her knife. Black and green filth exploded out of the eyeball onto both of them, and the beast let out a howl from its core. It dropped Peter's leg to bite at Maggie. She jumped back. Peter lifted up his sword and rammed it up through the jaw then pulled the blade out through the lip. The thing spun around and lacerated Peter's arm with its fin. Maggie jabbed her knife in its side and ran it right up the side like cutting through warm butter. The face kept going. It splashed around to bite at Maggie, but she stabbed it in the other eye. Peter ran up the side of a rock and, with a leap, swung the machete down right on its forehead. The beast shit out two little faces and then died, with its tongue hanging out of its mouth.

"Let's keep going," Maggie said, pulling Peter's hand. "No time to think about it."

Peter gazed at the giant dead face but nodded in agreement. "Yeah, no big deal. It's just…"

"It's just what?"

"Just…"

"What?"

"That face. It kind of…"

"Kind of what?"

"That face kind of looks like Mr. Calvo."

"Calvo. From chemistry?"

"Calvo from chemistry."

"Holy shit—the nose! It totally does!" Maggie snorted. "But hey…" She nudged him. "It's not. Come on."

Peter looked at her and then back at the face again. He took one more stab at it then started kicking his way through the remaining fish faces underfoot. They both kicked to the edge of the cavern, but they couldn't find any way out. The voices were so close they could almost hear what was being said. They heard a woman's voice, and maybe chanting. Then they heard a scream.

"That sounds like Jen!" Maggie said. "Shit, let's go back."

They both ran back the way they had come, kicking the fish faces out of their path until they were back in the tunnel.

49

Maria stood still and glared back with hatred at the bloated mass of evil that was Hosanna. The fire raged and the flames danced. Behind the hulking river queen mother, across the chaotic lashing surface of the dark lake, the pit of awful worshipers writhed and contorted in ways Maria had only heard of, but had never seen. The smoke swirled in thick plumes throughout the cavern, and the air was alive with the hot stench of rotting death.

"Your father was a fool," Hosanna said, as she accepted the help of her henchman back into her throne. She sat back and took a deep breath, looking content. "Kan B'alam thought he could come to this land and—what? Trick me?"

Maria felt her throat dry up, and her heart started racing.

"Yes," Hosanna said. "I know who you are. Do you really think I'd let you this close to me?"

"You will die in the mouth of your demon," Maria shrieked, bursting with full speed at the queen. She lunged at the queen, wielding a tiny dagger she had pulled from her thick black hair.

Joseph and the henchman moved with alarming speed and grabbed her, knocking her down to the bone-covered ground at the queen's feet. Max scrambled over and kicked the knife out of her hand.

The queen laughed deeply. "Children say the funniest things," she said flirtatiously to Joseph. "Pick her up and bring her to me."

They stood Maria up and jerked her in front of the queen's massive frame. Maria peered up over the enormous belly and breasts and folds of neck fat into her ancient enemy's hate-filled eyes.

"I know you just said that out of anger," Hosanna said, "but I can't allow you to blaspheme in this holy place."

"You worship the devil. There is nothing holy here."

"Be still, young one." She thrust out her fat hand and choked Maria. She lifted her tiny body off the ground, tightening her grip. Then she dropped her back down. "Don't talk anymore." She took another deep breath, her massive, naked chest heaving. "God has blessed my family. For a thousand years, God has granted my children eternal life. Look around you. Taste the life. Feel the life. Smell the life. Your family could have had it all. Look at my eyes, beautiful darling. Don't you see?" She leaned close. "Don't you see your father's eyes?"

Maria looked, and wept.

"You are one of us."

"No!"

"Shut up. Yes. You come from me. You descend from my blood. You descend from Axulche. Listen. Smell. This is your home. This is your life. You can live forever."

"I don't want to live forever! You kill babies. You killed your own babies and slept with your brothers and father and worship the devil!"

"What you call the devil is something so wonderful you don't understand. Can't you see the blessing bestowed upon us? Can't you see the sacrifice needed to have eternal life? To enjoy all of earth's pleasures? Heaven here on earth, inside the earth, in the earth."

"You're a monster. You killed my entire family line. We all lived here in peace. I know, I've read the runes. And you know too. You conjured the devil to kill your rivals."

"Ancient history."

"You never stopped killing! You killed my mother and father."

"They turned their back on God."

"There is no God. Only your pit from hell. And you're going in it tonight." Maria spat in the queen's face.

The queen lunged out of the chair but couldn't completely get out. The two men holding Maria pulled her back, and Joseph pried the queen's massive flab back out.

"Take her to the altar," the queen said, holding up the knife. "There is a God. And you will see him soon. You, of all people, should know the horrible countenance of his image."

Maria thought of her father. She thought about the countless nights poring over the histories. Learning the written language predating Sanskrit. Deciphering her family tree. Learning the art of war. She knew how to wield a sword before she knew how to ride a bike. She remembered what her father taught her about controlling her fear. Using her vulnerability as a weapon. She let them drag her over to the altar. She let them lift her up. She cleared her mind and thought of her mother's beautiful face, as they slammed her down on the jagged bone pile. Her pain registered, but her mind was focused. She screamed, but only to keep them comfortable.

Hosanna stood at the foot of the altar as the men held Maria down. Joseph and Max huddled behind their sister-mother queen. She grasped Maria's left ankle and lifted her leg up. She pulled off Maria's leather sandal. She chanted the ancient curse that had corrupted the deep waters for millennia. She swung the evil knife down and gouged into the base of Maria's foot. She hacked off her big toe. This time, Maria screamed for real. Hosanna popped the bloody nugget in her mouth and chomped down vigorously, cracking the bone in her rotten teeth. "Mmmh, oh my…" She chomped. "I've forgotten what K'inich virgin tastes like." She held her hand over her breast and fanned herself. "Ohh my, ohhh yes. Thank you, Lord."

Maria shrieked in terror, letting go of all her training as her survival instincts kicked in.

"You're delicious enough to be my own daughter," the queen cackled. "I could just eat you all up! Pity I can't." She looked across the water. "God is ready to receive you, my dear. My brothers and sisters have waited so long. You are the seventh. The final. The most pure of heart and pure of blood."

Joseph and Max crowded around the altar, kneeling and praying. The henchmen stepped back and kneeled as well.

"Seven prayers for seven cycles," the queen said. "One thousand years for every offering. One virgin for each millennium past, and one for each new dawn."

Maria lay across the altar, sobbing, bleeding out of her left foot. Hosanna lifted up her knife, rolled her eyes back, and started reciting the ancient hymn.

Then she heard a noise she wasn't expecting. It sounded like a chainsaw.

50

Jerrod and Beth exploded into the cavern like ber-
serker warriors from ancient times. Their eyes
bulged, insane with fury. They were drenched in sweat
and the ancient decay of the tunnels. Their minds
were ravaged by the death and violence that had torn
through their weekend. While running straight for the
writhing throng in front of him, Jerrod held the rusted,
bloody chainsaw high up in the air with both hands.
He revved it high as he sprinted toward the cursed
orgy. The hundreds of Hosanna's naked children
couldn't hear the menacing whine. They couldn't see
their dual angels of death rapidly approaching. Their
thoughts were all on Axulche, worshiping their dark
god as they ferociously penetrated each other. Beth
Miller swung the hatchet high above her filthy blond
hair, and together she and Jerrod Farina descended
on the horde.

51

The monstrous fish delivered Jen Miller's corpse, to join the five prior sacrifices, down into the black boiling water. The storm underwater raged, and the thousands of fish danced in celebration as their god stirred. The water turned purplish blue, and riptides coursed in all directions at once. The lake bottom was alive. Something was rupturing. The volcano of blood had torn a gaping maw in the blue, bubbling rock. The crevice spread wide in a twisted frown, and veins the size of tree trunks exploded out of the jagged black hole. The bloody tentacles shot up like a bullet train toward Jen's aquatic funeral procession. The veins reached her body two hundred feet from the lakebed. The gigantic eel-like appendages twirled around her body, and five of the catfish surrounded her. The thing held her momentarily in an almost graceful embrace, Jen's entrails and hair floating up in the burning water, and then instantly it pulled her down into the gaping hole it had come from.

The opening slammed shut like a gargantuan clam the size of a soccer field. The bubbling rock turned into explosions, and blue light pierced the dark water thousands of feet up. Volcanoes of blood and glowing blue ooze erupted in hundreds of spots, shooting horrid lava up, killing the catfish. The entire lake was boiling. More fish exploded, while others swam ferociously toward the surface. The volcanoes bubbled and spurted and rolled over into the liquid rock as the whole lakebed began to expand like a balloon, blowing up and rising up in the lake. Blue light blazed up from the bottom with the strength of a dying sun.

52

Jerrod attacked the first giant white ass he saw stick-ing up toward him. He drove the chainsaw right through the taint, and didn't stop until he lopped off a leg up to the pelvis. Excrement and blood splat-tered onto Jerrod's face. He laughed hysterically. Beth screamed her war cry and chopped her way toward the first neck she could come in contact with. She yanked out the hatchet and struck again and again until the head came right off. With her left hand, she grabbed the long hair of the woman and pulled as hard as she could, still swinging at the next naked person with her right. The mass of naked bodies kept fucking, oblivi-ous to the carnage around them. Their eyes were closed. Their minds were on their god of the deep. They prayed with fervor. They cried in ecstasy. They only cried in pain when the blade tore through their arms, faces, and spines. And when the long overdue hatchet was buried in their skull.

53

The queen saw her children dying on the other shore. She saw her defenseless babies brutally murdered, on this—the holiest of nights.

"Leave them alone!" she screamed across the cavern. "Stop them!" she commanded the men surrounding Maria. "Maxamilian! Joseph! Where are my boys?"

"They were at the gates, Mother," Max said. "They were guarding the gates."

She squinted at the glint of the chainsaw and the flowers of blood exploding onto the pristine white flesh of her family. "We will eat your faces!" she screamed. "And Axulche will steal your souls!"

She stormed over to the fire as two of her brothers and two of their children got onto the boat and rowed out into the glowing blue lake. The boat surged and dipped in the waves. The water burned as it splashed up on their skin. Hosanna waved her giant arms at the flames, conjuring them up, summoning all her ancient power. She was the strongest. Only she could lead her family on the path. Only she could speak with

Axulche. Only she could summon him when the planets aligned and the earth stood still on the longest day of the year, when the virgin blood of her own blood was shed, when the thousand orgasms were reached, when the vitality of a million babies was sucked out of the marrow, and when the pure virgin blood, at the peak of ripeness, was offered up.

"Axulche! Soet! Cuthsmx!" she chanted, her eyes rolling back.

Screams came from across the lake, blood and limbs exploding. She could see the girl that looked like her last sacrifice attacking a daughter, now a son. She looked at her brother's boat. It wasn't even halfway across. Her flock was getting killed. The lake grew brighter.

Change of plans, she thought. She urinated down her thigh. Smearing a droplet on her hand, she cast it into the fire. Then she pulled some filth from her backside and flicked that into the flames. Then she swallowed five times quickly in a row, convulsing her stomach. She threw up, projectile vomiting into the flames. Finally she cut her left hand and flung her blood into the fire. "Nusad kayl iuwr!" she cried.

The fire turned brown and shot up across the ceiling of the cavern. Thick smoke poured over her. She lifted up her hands and then stretched forward, eyes bloodshot and furious. The smoke shot out across the lake, launching the boat out of the water and sending it and the four passengers flying through the air to the other side. The smoke ripped into the crowd.

The queen stood leaning forward. She clenched her fists. The smoke contracted into a thick black ball, choking her children, choking Jerrod and Beth, thick in the lungs like mud. Then Hosanna, the evil queen, splayed her fingers wide open, and the smoke exploded through every orifice like a tornado guest. Instantly the horde stopped fucking. They stopped moving.

Jerrod staggered back. Beth fell down hard on the ground on her backside. Jerrod lifted her up, and the two took a step back. They were ten bodies deep into a countless crowd. As though moving with the will of single consciousness, the entire crowd opened their eyes at once. Then they slowly turned to face Beth and Jerrod. Old. Naked. Thousands of sagging breast and earlobes. Hundreds of blood-covered frowns. Almost all of them were stained with the blood and semen of their own siblings. The horrid throng stared at the pair. Then they all turned to look at the bodies of their mutilated brothers and sisters, cleaved on the floor in a still-growing pool of blood.

The queen held the middle finger of her left hand in her right. "Virtw xbne!" she seethed, and broke her finger completely.

The smoke squiggled inside her offspring, scurried up their spinal cords, and shot into their brains. Collectively, their eyes turned red. What white hair was left on their heads started moving like snakes up into the decrepit air. Their skin grew tight, their muscles bulged, they bared their teeth and howled a demonic chorus.

Beth ran at them first, and Jerrod followed one step behind. The naked children were wild with murderous rage. Blood filled their lust more than any sexual pleasure now. They prayed to their god by slaughter. They worshiped their earthly host by carnage and dining at the feast of gore. Jerrod swung the chainsaw through the jaw of the first attacker and into the cheek of the second. He lopped off hands, he crushed skulls. He swung the chainsaw into the breast of a skinny, old woman his grandmother's age, and through the stomach of a man and out his back, and tore into the guy behind him. Jerrod swung wildly, without aim, tearing through skin and flesh and muscle and bone and innards. Beth swung with fierce determination, but they descended on her too quickly. She kicked and hacked. Two, three, four more dead.

But they kept coming—kept pouring in on the two. Reaching and biting and grabbing and digging at them with their hardened claws. Pain had no meaning. Pain coursed through their veins now. Death had no meaning, just blood. Just meat from the mortals. Together they had lived one thousand years, and after tonight they would live one thousand more.

Jerrod jabbed the chainsaw into the neck of an attacker and chopped the legs off the next. Chopping and spinning, he cut his way into the crowd, mutilating any hand, foot, arm, leg, face, neck, head, or anything else that got within two feet of him. Beth was covered in blood. Rolling between two legs spread apart, she caught the edge of her weapon right between the legs of the woman standing over her. She jerked it as hard as she could, ripping off a chunk of flesh as she swung the hatchet into the next attacker's skull. She tugged the weapon back out as she kicked an oncoming attacker in the face. He fell backward, taking three behind him down. More poured in from all sides.

One got hold of Beth's hair and pulled her down. She swung wildly, using all her energy and hatred to fight. Her adrenaline was pumping like never before in her lifetime.

Beth and Jerrod spun in unison now, striking the insane mob, cutting together. Slaughtering in rhythm. Dancing the red death. Cleaving their way through. Beth didn't think of Scott. She didn't think of Jen. She didn't think of Jerrod. Beth thought of ending the lives of every naked, old monster she could get her hands on. I was born. Whack. To kill. Slurt. All of you. Flgght. The whine of Jerrod's chainsaw was her melody. When it connected with bone, it was the beat. She kept to the rhythm, hacking away. Showers of blood and guts and eyeballs and brains poured from every blow they connected. The fumes and the blood and the insane stench of death and revenge intoxicated Jerrod. Beth swung at her foes and laughed as she killed. She swung backhand and connected with a shoulder. And then she stopped. She felt something. She looked down. A dagger was stuck up to the hilt in her stomach. Holding the dagger was a grotesque midget. She tried to pull her hatchet loose but didn't have the energy. She sat down. The wild-haired flock didn't seem interested in her anymore. They were going over to play with Jerrod. Just this short little boy and me, she thought.

"What's your name?" Beth asked. She lay down.

"Maxamilian." The little boy lay down next to her and patted her head.

"Have you seen my sister?" she asked.

"A pretty young lady that looks like you?"

"Yes, that's her. Have you seen her?"

"Why, yes," said Max. "My sister…" He paused. "Can you see my sister way over there?"

He tilted her head to the side, so she faced the glowing, thrashing lake. The violence of the lake snapped her out of her delirium.

"I can see a fire and a big woman and a girl lying on something."

"Yes, that woman standing is my sister. She is our queen."

"But have you seen my sister?"

"Oh yes," Max said. "I saw her when my sister blessed her body and offered her up to God. She sliced your sister from her vocal cords to her vagina."

Beth turned to face the ugly midget, who laughed as he told her the news. She could see the chainsaw hacking off limbs behind them as more and more attackers descended on Jerrod. Max stood up and reached for his knife still stuck in her stomach. Before he could snatch it away, Beth pulled it out and buried it deep in Max's eye socket. She toppled him over, pulled herself up on him, and twisted his head around until his neck snapped. As she stole his dying breath, a pack of the naked, bloody, geriatric zombies broke off and descended on Beth. They tore into her back and bit into her neck and thighs and feasted on her body and Max's body below her. Beth was walking through a meadow in the foothills with her sister when her skull caved in and her brain spilled out into Max's mangled eyehole.

54

Peter instantly saw three things when he peered around the cavern entrance. He held Maggie back behind him as she ran up, so he could survey the war in front of them. The first thing Peter saw was the giant, naked woman across the lake doing something to a young girl. Was that Jen? No, it was the Mexican girl. The second thing he saw was the lake turning blue and going crazy, with fish jumping up out of the water, into the air and up on the rocks. The third thing he saw was Jerrod's chainsaw buzzing through a melee of what looked like aged medusas.

"Beth!" Maggie screamed.

Peter saw the carnage. The horde heard Maggie's yell and started running toward them. The old, skinny guy from the cabin was running toward them too. Peter ran with his machete outstretched. Maggie followed close behind. They collided with the naked beasts and chopped their way through to Jerrod. Jerrod saw the blood flowers coming toward him.

"Don't teach this in college, do they!" he shrieked. He slammed the chainsaw into a shoulder blade, and the teeth stuck. The blade stuck. He pulled it lose with both hands, and the wound kept hold of the chain. It finally broke. Jerrod looked at his rusted metal bar for a second and then started clubbing his attackers. They moved in closer now. "Get out of here, buddy!" he yelled. "You two go water skiing and have a beer on me!"

"We're not leaving you!" Peter yelled. "Hold on, you motherfucker!"

"I've killed so many of these cocksuckers, I'm getting the hang of it now!" Jerrod said, as one grabbed his arm and tore a huge cut through his forearm. "I've got this, don't even trip!"

"Jerrod!" Maggie screamed.

Jerrod hit one more elderly, blood-crazed, naked goon with the broadside of his worthless weapon, and then two grabbed him from behind. Two more got a hold of his legs. Even more gripped pieces of his hair and dug their claws into his stomach and chest, and they all pulled for their own taste, and Jerrod's entrails exploded onto their insane wrinkled faces.

Peter and Maggie stood in shock as they witnessed their friend eviscerated. Peter held up his machete in defense. Maggie stood by his side, knives drawn. They weren't being attacked. The zombies were all facing them. They were dropping down to their knees. Their eyes were losing their red glow. The white hair of the women was falling back down on their shoulders. They were all crying and laughing. They were bowing and crying and kneeling in prayer. Maggie tapped Peter's shoulder. He glanced to his side.

"What the fuck is it now?" he whispered.

"Look," she said.

Peter slowly looked behind him. A bright blue light was glowing. Then he turned completely around. He dropped his machete.

55

Peter and Maggie were almost blinded by the blue sun that rose up out of the water. The orb was covered in pulsing black and purple and red veins. Fish parts and whole fish, alive and dead, slid down its sides as the massive shape lifted up out of the water. It took up the entire stretch of the lake surface. It was an abomination. Terrible tongues protruded from the gaping hole that was the mouth of the creature. The tentacles flung wildly up in the air, hundreds of feet, searching, whipping through the cavern. The blue head expanded and broke apart the rocks on the shore like it was too big for the massive space it was squeezing through, up and up, filling the cavern space.

Peter picked his weapon back up off the ground as a catfish the size of a cow landed two feet away from them and splattered twenty feet in every direction. More fish, big and small, rained down on them, some landing on the worshipers and others splattering on the blood-covered rock surface like giant raindrops of fish guts. The smell filled Maggie with despair. The entire cavern shook. The naked cult sang in an ancient tongue and swayed their hands in the air as the demon rose from the depths of hell.

Axulche had awakened. Axulche was hungry. One horrible eye opened across fifty feet of rotten godflesh. The blood vein tongue struck down upon the congregation, grasping up twenty or more naked seniors. They broke from their trance and screamed as they hurtled through the air, crushed by the grip of the poisonous barbs sticking deep into their bodies. The massive gaping maw opened wide, and the tongue pulled them down into a pit of millions of razor-sharp shark teeth.

Peter grabbed Maggie to head back to the tunnel. She screamed. He looked back. An unbelievably long tentacle had wrapped around her ankle and was pulling her back. Thousands of veins tore through the cavern, searching for food, searching for flesh. The old people were running now, trying to push each other out of the way. Burning catfish parts rained down on all of them. Blood-covered veins hurtled through the crowd, tearing people limb from limb just by grazing their sides. Axulche burned with blue, glowing fire and glutted on the hundreds of easy targets. Peter hacked off the tentacle with his machete, but another one grabbed his arm. Scores of people were taken up in the air, some living, some dead, all thrown into the same horrible teeth of utter pain and suffering. Maggie scrambled toward the tunnel to escape, and Peter followed. Blocking the entrance, with an ax, was the old scab-covered man with the beard—Joseph.

56

Hosanna was convulsing as the demon's searing hide bulged and squirted up out of the lake. The ancient queen witch was chanting in a tongue long forgotten. Her eyes rolled back showing only the bloodshot whites. Her sweat and blood-covered breasts quivered and swung as she shook and trembled, invoking her god, praising him, loving him, giving over to him completely. She defecated and came as her body was possessed with the dim light of a million blinking souls. She felt her bones strengthen. Her hair grew long. Her breasts soared. With each terrified son or inbred daughter that was torn apart falling into her god's esophagus, Hosanna's terrible power grew. Her heart soared as Axulche feasted on her sacrifice. Her children. Her true sacrifice, her own blood, was offered in legion. The fire she had used to help conjure her savior from the depths was put out by hundreds of flailing fish, boiling alive, cascading off the glowing blue monolith.

Maria opened her eyes as she lay flat on the bone altar and immediately saw a hundred-pound bullhead catfish falling straight toward her. Its long whiskers fluttered in the hot air as it shot openmouthed for her face. She jerked up and rolled off the table of death just as the fish exploded where her head had been. Fish bombs went off all around her. She saw a brilliant blue, slime-covered wall rolling up. She looked up to the top of the cavern and saw the horizon of the beast and the tentacles fanned out like seaweed in a hurricane, whipping bloodstained victims up to the cavern ceiling hundreds of feet up and devouring them. She sidestepped another fin and tail disaster and turned to see Hosanna smiling and changing. She was singing, and she was radiating the same blue color as the monster boiling over the lake. Intense light was shooting out of her mouth and eyes and ears. The queen was shaking wildly and laughing. And she was growing with each body that was thrown into the beast's mouth.

Maria stared with absolute hatred at the evil whore who had ruined her family for millennia. Maria had one more knife tangled into her thick black curls—the knife her father had given her for her seventh birthday. The knife was short, but never grew dull. She pulled it from her long hair. Dots and dashes covered both sides. A sea serpent was carved into the hilt. She kissed the tip of the blade, drawing a drop of blood. She looked down at her foot. She had momentarily forgotten the pain. Now it came back, and for a moment, she felt the wave of fear and loss return. She remembered her father. She remembered her mother. She remembered her great grandmother telling her the ancient truth. She remembered her breathing. She swallowed. She walked forward slowly, knife tucked in hand.

Instantly the glowing queen whipped toward her.

"You're too late," Hosanna said. "Bow down in terror at your God!" she screamed. The god was tearing through the fleeing mass, bellowing with a deep croak from hell. Hundreds killed, hundreds eaten.

"You said they would live forever!" Maria screamed over the wailing and screaming and the wind and fish and bowel-shaking vibrations emanating from the beast.

"They will live forever," the queen said. "In me! Don't you understand? This is my blessed sacrifice! It is through the blood of my children that Axulche can drink of the life of the earth and let me taste his teardrop. It is through the blood of my brothers and sisters that I reign for a thousand years. A thousand more I shall rule. For tonight God has eaten, and he blesses me now. For I am his bride!"

"Murderer!" Maria yelled, jumping aside as a tentacle whipped past her leg. She didn't take her eyes off the obese queen. "You will suffer in hell for eternity!" She ran fast, jumping over giant bloody veins and fish everywhere, snapping and exploding.

The queen summoned more of the tentacles, and the blue wall shifted and started falling toward Maria as she ran. She flipped out her knife. The queen recognized the blade—forged from bone at the mouth of the bottomless pit below. The knife she herself had used to make her first sacrifice on this most important day of the year, six thousand years ago. She conjured all her demonic power and begged her god to kill the young descendent of her long-dead sister.

Maria leapt over the charred remains of the humans Hosanna had engorged herself on. The queen screamed, excrement pouring down her inner thighs. Maria took two more steps and then soared through the air as a dozen tentacles grabbed for her. She landed on Hosanna and drove the white hellfire knife deep into the queen's fat neck. She pulled it out, and blue blood shot out twenty feet up in the air. She stabbed the top of Hosanna's left breast and then stabbed again. The queen punched her, and Maria bounced off, but she pulled the knife down hard and tore a deep gash straight down to the queen's hairy, grotesque nipple. Maria somersaulted to one side, jabbed the knife in the queen's fat stomach, and then pushed hard and ran around the front to the other side. The blade wasn't long enough to cut through the fat. The queen lumbered around, knocking her to the ground with her giant fist.

"I'm immortal!" Hosanna screamed, her hair writhing in demonic fury. "You can't kill me! No one can kill me! I am the lover of Axulche! The provider of the feast! Through Death I am Life!" Blue light and blood poured from every cut and orifice.

Maria scrambled back and stared as the queen towered over her. She looked as horrible and terrifying as the ancient demon behind her. Almost. The queen stretched out her fat arms to kill Maria, her pathetic rival. Maria pushed back farther but backed up into the cave wall. The queen beamed with blinding light. Maria saw more tentacles. They surrounded and wiggled behind the queen. They were all around the queen. Bloody veins were nipping at the wounds she had made with her knife. More were hovering around the queen, tongues lapping her blue-and-red ooze. The queen paused her attack and batted one away. Another one pecked her breast where the giant tear was. The barbs of the tentacle tugged at the raw flesh. The queen turned around, waving them off with her ham hands. She turned and saw the fifty-foot eye of a creature that had seen dinosaurs. She screamed. One hundred flesh-lusting tongues attached to her meaty frame, and all joined in to lift her off the ground. She wailed. The eye was blinking furiously, and the one blue head in the cavern, out of the demon's thousands, convulsed and rippled with excitement. Hosanna felt the age of a million deaths rip through her as the sharp barbs cut though her skin and fat. She was hoisted up to the roof of the cavern, high above the horrible hole where her children now writhed and screamed. They were living and dead, all together, screaming and bleeding and cut in half and more parts, reaching up for help, crying to any god other than the one they thought would give them life. The living saw their mother coming to join them and reached up to welcome her. Their hatred and love and fear and rage ripped through them collectively, and they scrambled up out of the pile of human carnage to pull her down to join them. Her grown children's hands and teeth ripped her from the demon's tongues and tore her apart. She screamed one last cry, and the last of the blue light faded in her and was covered and put out by brown and black and red and fat and bone and brain and shit and baby livers inside her stomach, and a mess of human arms and legs and bodies writhed around and sang out of fear and unholy pain and terror.

57

Joseph stood at the mouth of the tunnel, guarding the passageway. Peter didn't have time to stop. Hundreds of naked geezers were running up behind him. Tentacles groped and curled in every direction. Joseph clawed wildly at them both. Peter struck him down with one machete chop. Joseph fell to the ground. Maggie stomped his head as she jumped over him. Peter jumped into the cavern, turned around, and then swung the machete down once more. The blade cut through Joseph's neck and tore right through to the floor. He kicked the body out of the tunnel and into the path of the oncoming hoard. As the throng reached the cave mouth, Peter hacked off a limb of each person that got close. Tentacles grabbed the pale, naked prey and ripped them up into the air. Peter and Maggie fought them back, each one, chopping and stabbing and slaughtering human and monster alike to protect their escape.

Then the tentacles fell away. The horrible groaning had stopped. The shouting and screaming had stopped. A pile of old people lay dead at their feet, and hundreds more behind them. One man limped toward them. It was a naked, old man with a buzz cut. His face was covered in blood.

"Hey, you two," Bill said. "Thank God almighty." He paused behind the body of corpses piled up. "What a royal snafu!"

"Stay back, motherfucker!" Maggie warned. "Why aren't you wearing any clothes?"

"Well, funny story. Jesus H. Christ, look at this mess." He kicked one of the limbs away and hobbled a little closer. "Maybe I can borrow some of your clothes, and we can kind of head back up to the ol' marina. What do you say, kids? I can fix us up some nice…"

Maggie's knife flew from her fingers and found purchase right between his eyes. He farted, and died as he hit the ground. They both watched for movement, but there was none.

"Hey, where did the giant fucking fish monster go?" Peter said, realizing the giant blue monster was gone.

Maggie fell into his arms. Peter dropped his machete and gave her the strongest embrace he could remember. She pulled back and looked into his eyes.

"Peter Rockwood. Holy crap."

"No shit. I love you, babe."

"Love you, babe."

The two kissed, deeply and warmly, ignoring the gore caked to their faces. They finally stepped away and surveyed the devastation.

"Are we in hell?" Peter said.

"I think we're at the north entrance."

58

Maria stood by the altar and witnessed her great-grandfather's father's grandfather's sworn enemy's demise—the evil queen that had been written about for so many generations. The hideous witch who killed so many innocents was dead.

She was gone.

She's gone, Father.

She's gone, Grandfather.

She's gone, Mother.

She dropped the knife. She watched as the demon's blue glow dimmed, and the black hulking mass receded back into the lake. The tentacles disappeared back into the hole. The groaning croak shaking the cavern stopped. The mass dropped faster now, sending water spraying up throughout the cavern. In seconds, it was gone completely, and a terrific wall of death-soaked water splashed up to the rocky ceiling. The water came crashing down, drenching Maria where she stood. Waves reverberated, but the water wasn't burning anymore. Across the lake, all she could see were dead bodies. She stared blankly at the water and then slowly looked up again at the cavern ceiling, at the hole where the first rays of sun were starting to shine in from the east. She gazed at the intricate runes chiseled into the rock walls impossibly high above her head. Maria touched her fingertips to the inscriptions carved into the rock wall behind her. She could read the symbols. She could hear them whisper to her. They whispered from countless lost generations. They sang in a soft whisper in her ear. The beautiful voices were her grandmothers and aunts and great-grandmothers. They sang to her. They sang her name. It was the most beautiful sound she had ever heard. She fell to her knees and wept.

59

"Look!" Peter pointed across the piles of carcasses, across the fish guts and heads strewn about the stone floor. As the sun shone through the gap in the ceiling high above them, across the still water of the black lake, a little girl sat huddled by herself.

"Hey!" Maggie called. "Are you all right?"

The little girl lifted her head. She wiped away tears. Then she waved and smiled.

"Stay there, we'll come get you!" Peter said. He found the battered wooden boat flipped over by the shore.

Maggie helped him right it. She got in with the stern in the water, and Peter pushed it out and then joined her. The water was still, with bits of gruesome remains floating here and there, but no sign of life. He rowed them across safely. He stepped out of the boat, helped Maggie out, and they both hurried to the girl's side.

"I'm Peter. This is Maggie. What's your name?"

"Maria."

"Are you okay? Are you hurt?"

"Just my toe." Maria pointed.

"Jesus," Peter paused. "Gosh…I mean…that had to hurt."

"Yeah, it did."

"Did your dad…"

Maria shook her head.

"Sorry. I thought that was you. I'm so sorry, Maria." Maggie hugged her. Maria let her.

"What about that giant fat thing that was by you? Did she do that to your toe?"

Maria nodded.

"Where is she?"

"She drowned."

"Good. Let's get out of here, before she pops back up out of the water. What do you say?" Peter said. "You two ready to go?"

Maria took one last look at the remains of the ancient ziggurat. She listened to the cheery voices swirling around her that these two obviously couldn't hear. She nodded her head. Maggie helped her to the boat. Peter pushed off once more. They rowed out across the lake of death. The sun shone brightly into the cavern, revealing ancient art and arcane symbols covering every square foot of the massive natural canvas. The cave of the blue sea demon, Peter thought. The cave of a million dying breaths.

Peter carried Maria on his back as they waded through the piles of dead corpses and the blood and carnage where they had battled for their lives. They hiked through the crystal caves. They crawled through the narrow tunnels. They passed through the hall of doors where the brothers' remains festered with engorged, slithering scavengers. Maggie and Peter crawled up the spiral staircase, completely exhausted. Even with one toe missing, Maria bounded up the steps, yearning for the sunlight. They climbed for what seemed like hours, until they finally reached the top, and fell through the tiny doorway into the back of the cabin. They ran outside into the fresh morning air. They fell to the dirt, laughing and crying. The sun blazed out of the east in the already hot Midwest air. Peter kissed the ground. Maggie rolled through the grass over to him and kissed him.

"Have you two ever had sex?" Maria asked, standing behind them on the porch. Peter rolled off Maggie to look at her.

"What kind of question is that for a little girl?" Maggie asked.

"Great-grandmother wants to know."

Peter lifted himself up on his elbows. "Great-grandmother?"

"You two look like you have had sex. You have, right?"

"Well, yeah, but…"

"That's okay. Just wondering."

"You must be in shock." Maggie stood up and walked over to comfort her. "You want a drink of water? We can go find some."

"Water?" Maria said. "I want your blood!" she shrieked, lunging for Maggie's face. Her fingernails dug into Maggie's eyeballs, and she stabbed Maggie in the heart with her dagger.

"No!" Peter yelled, running to his lover's side. Maria had already mortally wounded her, and she jumped to meet Peter head-on. She stabbed him in the stomach as he closed in on top of her and then bit his face. She flew into a fury, her hair whipped around in the air. Her eyes grew red, and she bit and clawed and chewed her way through his chest cavity and feasted on the organs inside.

60

The voices sang in a deafening chorus in her ears. They chanted and warmed her heart and made her giggle and laugh at the fond memories of her beautiful family. You're on the start of a wonderful journey, they sang. You are the living legend. You are walking the path danced by the first women under the moon. You are tracing our path through the ages. As the moon and the stars glide through the night into eternity, so will you glide through the days and the river and the rock. Praise be to the one who can lay the bounty before God and feed him with her hands. Praise be to the feast that you have served to our king. Praise be to all creatures, swimming, running, and singing.

She prayed with them as she feasted, growing stronger and wiser with every slurp. This can't be virgin meat, she thought. But it would suffice. She'd taste one soon enough.

The River Princess had plenty of time to kill.

The End

Frank Young was born in 1974. After growing up on the Rock River, Young left for the mountains of Colorado, where he drank whiskey and got into street fights. He moved to Chicago fourteen years and a few scars later to work as a newspaperman.